The Haunting of Gothia/Rebecca

BY
Marsha Hubbard Norton Ketih

CHAPTER I

The real estate agent seemed to give Gothia a look that said you are kidding, when Gothia asked to see the house on Hollow Lane.

Whether it was her name or her clothes Gothia was not sure why she was getting the look she was getting from the real estate agent.

Gothia was not her real name, but as a writer of Gothic and Paranormal romance the name Rebecca Miller just did not seem to fit so the name Gothia was born.

It also helped in her writing that in her younger days the Goth's were her group. She wore the clothes, the make-up and listened to the music.

Even now at age 26 she still liked most of the clothes, but she leaned more to what the real Goth enthusiast wore: the 18th and 19th century period clothes. Gothia knew her black crushed velvet jacket with a white ruffled shirt was getting a look from the real estate agent. The tight fitting jeans and black ankle boots help to set off the outfit and gave her a unique look.

Gothia's long, black hair hung loose and the one strand she had frosted silver stood out vividly.

The effect was startling to some she knew, but she dressed for herself not others. The fact that she got many admiring glances from men did not impress her at all.

"Are you sure you want to see the house on Hollow Lane?" asks the real estate agent again.

"Oh yes, I drove by and found it by accident," says Gothia, "and---

"But it is an awfully old house and quite big," interrupts the real estate agent. "I do have some very nice smaller houses and even a few condos in your price range."

Condos, thinks Gothia, the kind upper income, conservative people like, well that is not I.

"No Hollow Lane please, I like the old and big part," says Gothia as she walks toward the front of the real estate office.

CHAPTER II

As they pulled up to the house on Hollow Lane, Gothia felt as if she has come home.

Whatever wrong turn took her to this street was a blessing as far as Gothia was concerned. But, as Gothia was a strong believer in fate, she felt this was fate for her to find this house.

The lawn needed a little work with the yard needing a mowing and the bushes needing a trim as well as a once beautiful rose garden now overgrown with weeds.

The house itself needed some paint and a few boards replaced but otherwise looked sturdy with the roof having been replaced in the last five years according to the real estate agent.

As they walk onto the porch Gothia feels a sense of peace, but she also feels some thing else.

A sudden breeze blows across the porch and a wisp of hair blows into Gothia's face.

As she moves her hair back Gothia swears she can smell Old Spice, something her grandfather use to wear.

"Okay if you are sure," says the real estate agent as she puts the key into the front door lock.

"I am sure," says Gothia.

As the real estate agent opens the front door, Gothia gasps in pleasant surprise.

The foyer is big and a spiral staircase greets Gothia's eyes. It winds up to the second floor of the house.

The house looks as if it was built in the late 1800's if not the early 1900's.

"Oh it is beautiful," says Gothia as she moves farther into the house and then into a room that looks like it must have been the formal living room.

"Yes it is. The house was built over a hundred years ago as it was built in 1900. Through the years some modernizations have been made but the basic structure is the same," says the real estate agent as they move to another room, which appears to have been the library.

Bookshelves line the walls and reach up to the ceilings. A large crystal chandelier sits in the center of the library.

Oh this room is beautiful, I could not even begin to fill these shelves, thinks Gothia as she twirls around the room, but I would love to try.

"How many rooms does this house have exactly," asks Gothia as she and the real estate agent move back to the foyer.

"Downstairs you have the formal living room, the library, and a formal dining room, kitchen and one bathroom. There is also a screened in porch that is off the back of the house and off the kitchen you will find a large laundry room that was put in some time in the 60's. That room used to be the cooks bedroom I think. Upstairs you have five bedrooms with three bathrooms, one that is off the master bedroom.

"Wow, five bedrooms," says Gothia as they move to the kitchen.

"Yes and out back is a two car garage with a small apartment over it that would make a nice potential second income, renting it out."

"Maybe," says Gothia. But, more of an idea was to offer it to some of her writing friends down on their luck.

The kitchen is large and has the look of an older period of time. A large gas oven takes up one wall with a more modern refrigerator and freezer on the other wall. The sinks are now stainless steel instead of the porcelain of the early 1900's.

"Shall we go upstairs," asks the real estate agent as she and Gothia move back to the foyer.

"Yes of course," replies Gothia as the real estate agent leads the way upstairs.

As they move up the stairs Gothia imagines what the house may have looked like when it was new. The wall along the staircase shows signs where pictures hung.

Gothia can picture the formal parties with women in their long flowing gowns and the men in their formal suits. The band plays music of the time and the food and wine flow freely.

"Do you have any history of the house?" asks Gothia as they move from one bedroom to another. The modernization of the house is very evident in the bathrooms with new tubs and sinks as well as new tile. Luckily the bedrooms had only been modernized by the installing of the central air and heat as well as ceiling fans.

"As you can see the house has had central air and heat installed but it also has three working fireplaces. One in the living rooms and library as you saw and one in this room," says the real estate agent as she opens what must be the master bedroom.

Gothia cannot help but notice the agent has not heard or is ignoring her question about the history of the house.

The master bedroom is large and the walls are covered in a pale green paint and wood around the bottom is dark. The lighting is the ceiling fan with three lights. A fireplace centers one wall of the master bedroom and the mantle is white marble.

"This room is lovely," says Gothia as they move to the hall.

"I was wondering if you know any of the house's history," asks Gothia again as they move to the hallway.

"The history of the house," repeats the real estate agent

The look on her face makes Gothia wonder. It seems she wants to avoid the question of the history of the house.

As they stand in the hall Gothia sees a set up stairs she had originally missed. They seemed to lead to a third floor the real estate agent did not mention.

"Where do those stairs lead," asks Gothia as she points to the small narrow staircase. "I did not realize there was a third floor."

"Yes the gable is at the back of the house so you would not see it from the street. But all that is up there are the attic and one small room. The owner used it for storage I believe," says the real estate agent.

"I would like to see it anyway," says Gothia.

"Well, as you see the stairs are quite narrow," says the real estate agent.

"That is fine I can go up by myself," says Gothia, as she understands the woman might not want to maneuver the stairs, as she is somewhat bigger than Gothia.

"Well, the room is kept locked," says the real estate agent.

Her tone tells Gothia that she is reluctant to show the room and this makes Gothia want to see it even more.

If I did not know better I would think the woman was afraid, thinks Gothia as she watches the real estate agent twirl the keys in her hand.

"Well. I assume you have the keys to all parts of house," says Gothia. The woman's behavior makes her even more determined to see this room.

"Well, yes of course," says the real estate agent, her eyes not on Gothia but on the stairs that lead to the attic room.

"Okay give me the key to the room and I will go by myself," says Gothia as she holds her hand out.

As the real estate agent realizes she has no option but to give the key to her she hands the keys to the house to Gothia.

As Gothia walks up the stairs she glances back to see the real estate agent at the bottom of the stairs. The look on her face seems to be one of apprehension and worry to Gothia.

What can the woman be so afraid of wonders Gothia as she puts the key in the lock.

The lock did not look that rusty but it seemed to want to resist turning for Gothia. As the lock finally gives a click, Gothia feels a cool breeze against her cheek. The feeling is almost like a caress and the smell of Old Spice seems to fill her nostrils.

That was weird, thinks Gothia as she enters the room.

The room is great thinks Gothia as she moves toward the center of the room.

The ceiling is low but not so low that Gothia cannot stand in the center. Her head is about two feet below the ceiling.

As she looks around the large attic room Gothia is surprised to see some items in the room.

On closer inspections she sees a large wardrobe standing against one wall. It is at least a hundred years old, thinks Gothia.

What a waste, it is just sitting here gathering dust, thinks Gothia as she opens one of the wardrobe drawers. The drawers seem empty until Gothia looks closer.

The edge of a picture peeks our from under the lining of the drawer. As Gothia pulls on the picture she feels the cool breeze again and the scent of after-shave again fills her nose.

Okay there is no way there can be a breeze, thinks Gothia as she looks around the dusty, closed attic. And there is sure no way there can still be the scent of Old Spice here.

The picture is of a young couple and is dated August 1900. The picture is in black and white as it is so old, but even as old as it is Gothia can see the man is handsome. His hair is black and a little long for that time period but yet stylish. He is dressed in formal wear, his arm around a young woman and his other hand on the top of a cane. As she looks closer Gothia can see the head of the cane is a wolf's head.

As Gothia looks at the woman, she feels a shock through her whole system. The woman looks like me, thinks Gothia, but that is impossible. Her hair is dark and pulled back in the 1900's fashion. Two curls line the sides of her face. Her dress is long, the hem touching the top of her shoes

The look in the man's eyes as he looks down at the young woman tells Gothia how much he loves her.

Gothia runs her fingers across the couple's faces as she puts the picture back in the drawer

As she walks toward the door that must lead to the small room the real estate agent Gothia sees the only piece of furniture left in the attic room is a large oval mirror. The mirror looks as old as wardrobe and the glass is dusty and frame is tarnished, but it is still a lovely antique as far as Gothia is concerned.

Oh my lord, thinks Gothia as she opens the door to the small room. It looks as if she has stepped into the past.

A cast iron bed is still set up in the room. It has a mattress and pillows. All of which are covered with a quilt that looks to be very old.

As Gothia sits on the bed a thin layer of dust fills the air and Gothia sneezes.

Beside the bed sits a small table that is as old as the bed and on the table sits a porcelain pitcher and bowl.

How did the people who lived here in the past just leave these things here, wonder Gothia as her attention is drawn to a closet? Its door blends so well with the walls were it not that she was so observant Gothia would have missed seeing the door.

As she pulls on the closet door she finds it locked or stuck shut with age. Now this is weird, thinks Gothia as she tries to pull on the closet door once more. As it won't budge Gothia decides to stop struggling with it.

I will have to ask about a key for this closet, thinks Gothia as she goes around and looks at the pictures on the wall. Pictures she had ignored till now.

Two of them are floral drawing done by an amateur hand, but good, thinks Gothia. The third and last picture is that of the young woman in the old photo.

She is dressed in a dress that is very formal and more than likely used for a formal dance or ball.

I can't help it she looks like me or should I say I look like her, thinks Gothia as she runs her fingers over the painting.

She looks happy yet there is some thing else in her eyes.

"You are here, you have come back," says a voice behind Gothia. "What!" exclaims Gothia as she twirls around.

As she sees no one there, Gothia laughs.

Okay your imagination is on over drive, thinks Gothia, but some thing inside her tells her the voice was real. But for some reason she feels no fear.

As she goes to pull the door shut Gothia looks around the attic room once more.

Okay, this is for me, thinks Gothia as she heads down the stairs to tell the real estate agent her decision.

As Gothia gets to the second floor she does not see the real estate agent so she moves on down to the first floor.

Gothia can hear the real estate agent's voice coming from the kitchen so moves toward it. As she enters the kitchen she sees the real estate agent is on the phone.

"Yes, she went up stairs. I know she won't take this house now, but I wish she would," whispers the real estate agent.

Gothia realizes the woman does not know she is in the room and also wonders why she and the person she is on the phone thinks she won't take the house.

"Excuse me," says Gothia as loud as she can.

"I have to go, bye," says the real estate agent as she clicks her phone shut.

"Oh, I am sorry I was talking to the office," says the real estate agent. The look on her face seems to be one of embarrassment and worry to Gothia.

"That is fine and as I did hear your conversation I will tell you that you have nothing to worry about as I will take the house."

"You will! Even after going upstairs—oh I mean great. We can go to the bank now if you have time. I have all the paper work in my brief case and I am sure you will have no trouble financing this home. The price has been reduced drastically."

The look on the real estate agent's face seems to be one of relief at a sale more than happiness.

"Yes, I was wondering about that. Is there some thing wrong with wiring or plumbing?
I also asked you about the history of the house earlier but you seem to want to avoid the question."

"Oh, that was not it at all. I must not have heard you," says the real estate agent. The reason the house is so low is that the bank repossessed it when the owner turned it back in and we bought it at a bank sale. So my partners and I would like to see the house go. The wiring and plumbing are fine, we have had it all inspected."

"Well what can you tell me about the history of the house? How many owners has it had? That is the kind of history I would like to know if that is possible?"

"Well, I really don't know that much. The Stephen Edwards built the house in 1900. Shortly after it was built the house was sold.

"I see," says Gothia. Something inside her tells that the real estate agent is not telling her the whole story, but as the women seems to want to keep it quiet, Gothia decides she will let it rest.

I can research the house after I move in, thinks Gothia as the real estate agent moves toward the front door.

"I have all the paper work in my briefcase, so if you want me can go back to the office and fill it out. I am sure you will have no problem with the down payment," says the real estate agent as she waits for Gothia to exit the house.

As Gothia turns to give the house one more look she swears she can see a wisp of smoke move down the staircase, it seems to form the shape of a man.

Okay girl, thinks Gothia, curb your imagination.

As the real estate agent locks the front door, Gothia knows she has found her home.

CHAPTER III

As Gothia watches the movers work she thinks over the last few weeks. The sell went fine and very fast in Gothia's opinion. The price of the home was so reasonable or so low that Gothia was able to pay for the house in full.

It paid to be frugal with your money girl, thinks Gothia as she watches the movers move another load off the truck.

"Ma'am," says one of the movers. As he stands there he holds a large picture of the ocean in his hands. The colors are dark and brooding as the picture depicts a storm at sea.

"Ma'am," says the mover again. "Where does this go?"

"That goes in the library," answers Gothia.

"It's kind of gloomy," says the young mover.

"Oops sorry ma'am," says the mover as he sees the look on Gothia's face.

"No, it is fine, it is kind of gloomy. An old friend of mine painted it, he was kind of gloomy himself," says Gothia as she thinks about Eric.

She and Eric had met in college. They both were juniors. Rebecca came to the university from a small New York Junior College and Eric a private college in Europe. He was an art major while she was an English Lit and Creative Writing major.

They met at a local coffee shop frequented by a lot of the college students from the Arts Department.

Eric was sketching at his table and when Gothia glanced over his shoulder she realized he was sketching her.

At first she was irritated but then they began to talk. They seem to click from the start. They both looked a little odd with Gothia or Rebecca as she was called then in her Goth clothes and Eric in his out dated hippie look.

They both were brilliant students, but their philosophy on life and art was considered unique and even weird at times.

Then in their senior year they moved in together. Eric pushed for marriage but Rebecca was not ready. Eric was a loving and gentle lover, but he also had his dark side as Rebecca soon discovered.

He never was cruel but about two weeks after she had moved in with him Rebecca saw one of his dark, brooding moods.

At first she passed it off as his artistic temperament, after all she got really quiet when she in the middle of a writing project. But, Eric's moods were more than this.

Eric liked people to think he was a poor, starving student. But, unlike Rebecca who was going to college on grants and scholarships as well as working part time, Eric's family was very wealthy.

Eric resented them for it some times but he also enjoyed not having to work as it gave him more time to do his art as well as play the starving, misunderstood artist. He never liked talking about his family or even seeing them, but his father required Eric to make a monthly trip to see them in Long

Island, that is if he wanted to keep his monthly allowance check and his education paid for and of course he did.

After meeting his family for the first time Rebecca could see why he hated the visits. Eric's father was a successful corporate attorney while his mother enjoyed attending club meetings and going to the country club to meet friends for a drink or to a formal dance held there.

Their house was a mansion as far as Rebecca was concerned with a pool, a game room and six bedrooms.

Eric's father never said much as Eric was their only child, but Rebecca knew he hated the idea of Eric majoring in Art. He never missed a chance to try and get Rebecca to get Eric to change his major. He let her know he did not care if meant paying for eight more years.

When Rebecca told him she would not do this, as she knew Eric loved his art, Eric's father grew cool and distant to her. Her visits to them were strained as neither Eric's father or mother spoke to her much.

It got so that Eric's complaining about his family wore on Rebecca's nerves. It especially got to her after a full day of classes and eights hours at the coffee shop. There were a few times she had to curb her tongue so she would not tell him to shut up.

But with all his money and other privileges Rebecca knew her life was better than Eric's life and he knew it too.

Rebecca's parents were both middle class working people with her dad being a foreman at a glass factory and her mother working at a daycare. They were not rich but Rebecca had a home, clothes and two parents who encouraged her in writing. Her parents taught her to respect people and treat everyone equal. Her father told her they use to have relatives that were rich but this was a long time ago and the Wall Street Crash of the twenties took what money they had. Her father used to fill her heads with the stories of his ancestors; one he told her was murdered a hundred years ago. As she loved to read and write paranormal stories Gothia ate this one story up.

Her parents encouraged to write and were proud when she won a scholarship to junior college then senior college. They even tolerated her love for Goth clothing and her music. They never worried about her drinking or using drugs.

To this day she never touched more than a glass of wine.

Eric seemed jealous of her relationship with her family, but not jealous enough to try and do it on his own.

Eric's moods got more erratic the longer they lived together.

Rebecca would come home some times after a day of classes and work to find Eric sitting in a dark apartment, his gloomy music playing on the stereo and Eric at his desk with only a desk lamp to illuminate his drawings. His drawings on the desk were even somewhat depressing and macabre to Rebecca. The pictures were mostly in black and depicted pictures of death by suicide. When he was like this Rebecca could do nothing to cheer him and knew she just had to wait it out.

When he was in a normal state of mind, Eric's paintings were more color. They still depicted some gloom but not like those when he was in his dark mood. At these normal times he was loving and gentle and good to be with.

But, the moods became darker after the first semester of their senior year and Rebecca found it too painful to see him like this.

It was that this time that Rebecca began to suspect that Eric was experimenting with drugs. He still attended classes but only enough to pass. It was also at this time he discovered a group of new friends. Friends he told Rebecca he had met at the coffee shop, but Rebecca wondered if they were not his drug buddies.

Rebecca tried talking to Eric about them but he would get irritated and would tell her they were fine and were the only ones who understood him.

This really hurt Rebecca as she really cared for Eric.

Now today even years after it was all over it still hurt but Rebecca realized that she cared for, liked and even felt sorry for Eric but she never loved him, not really.

The closer it got to graduation the weirder and moodier Eric got. He was now taking to staying away from the apartment for days at a time.

Rebecca heard from mutual friends that Eric was still attending classes but a lot of the times he seemed spaced out during most of the classes.

One day after three days absence from the apartment Eric showed up at the apartment. He had dark circles under his eyes and had on the same clothes he had left in three days ago. He smelled like booze, cigarettes and sex if sex smelled.

When Rebecca confronted him about his absence and appearance Eric lost it with her.
He began to scream and her and then he began to throw things. Rebecca felt afraid of Eric for the first time in their relationship.

Just as Rebecca thought he might hit her, Eric got it together long enough to stop.
As Eric ran out of the apartment Rebecca knew it was over. She could not live like this.

On the day of graduation a package arrived for Rebecca. As she opened it the ocean scene greeted her, beautiful yet sad and scary. It was dark, turbulent and she knew with out reading the card that accompanied it that it was from Eric.

The note was brief but very upsetting to Rebecca.

It read: Dear Rebecca this is for you with my deepest apology. We have been good together but I am lost and feel I cannot come back to where I was. I hope your life is good and happy. It was signed Eric, nothing more than Eric

Eric was not at the graduation. Rebecca feared he would not be; but was still disappointed when he was not.

Rebecca tried calling his parent but they were cool and aloof and told her that there son had moved on. He did not feel the need to attend the graduation and she need to get over it and him. His mother even had the nerve to insinuate she was just after Eric's money.

After graduation Rebecca found a job quickly. She went to work for a publishing company in Massachusetts.

The job was interesting and still gave her enough time to do her own writing. It was also close to her parents in Connecticut.

About three weeks into the job Rebecca began to dream of Eric. The dreams were always the same; short but sad. The dreams seem to tell her that Eric was not only lost to her but to everyone else.

A week later Rebecca received a call from a former college classmate and one who had been a friend of Eric in Europe and here. He told her he had been trying to find her for a week.

Before he told her Rebecca knew Eric was dead.

The friend told her they had found his body at his family's beach house. The friend told her the room was full of art, art Eric must have done for weeks.

An empty bottle of pills were found by his body and a short note saying he was no longer lost.

Rebecca immediately called his family but was told the funeral had happened already and she was not informed as she was not welcome, then his mother hung up on her.

Rebecca grieved for a long while and when his family paid to have Eric's art put on display at a private show she went. Rebecca expected a cool reception but not the reception she got.

Eric's mother ordered her from the show and Eric's father sided with his wife but in a quieter tone.

When Rebecca tried to talk to her about Eric, Eric's mother went ballistic and screamed that Rebecca was the reason Eric was dead and that she knew Rebecca had been using him and they wanted the painting that had been delivered to her by courier.

Rebecca left the show but kept the painting.

Eric's mother threatened a lawsuit but once she saw the note from Eric the subject was dropped and Eric's painting and last gift stayed with her.

"Ma'am, ma'am we have moved it all in," says the young man who had moved the painting in. The look in his eyes told Gothia she had been out of it for a while.

"Oh thank you," says Gothia as she realizes that she had been standing still for at least fifteen minutes. The movers had worked around her and moved in the last of her stuff.

As the movers pull away Gothia spins in a circle. Her arms outstretched and hair blowing in the wind.

Her spot gives her a view of across the street and Rebecca sees a neighbor standing across the street staring at her.

"Hello," calls out Gothia as she waves. Gothia laughs as the neighbor turns quickly and goes back into her house.

I guess she thinks she has a weird neighbor, thinks Gothia as she turns to go back into her new home.

As she walks into the house Gothia feels a sense of joy and some thing else as a breeze flits across her face. A breeze with no source, thinks Gothia as all the windows are still closed.

CHAPTER IV

I need furniture, thinks Gothia as she walks into the living room. Her couch, which always seemed so large in her apartment, now seemed too small. Its color blended with the dark colors of the walls, as did her love seat and armchair. Her old fashion rocker and wood end tables with their Victorian lamps looked good in the house.

Over the fireplace here in the living room is where Eric's picture needs to go not the library, thinks Gothia as she moves to the library. Her collection of 200 books would do little to fill the shelves in the library.

As Gothia rummages through the boxes she finds copies of her books. With six books to her name Gothia saw very decent royalties. Her publisher was pushing her for her next book, but for once the book was not coming.

As she moves from room to room Gothia plans her new ideas for her house.

Moving from one bedroom to the next upstairs Gothia thinks, Lord five bedrooms what was I thinking? I have one bedroom set. Well, I never had much need for more.

Having kids was something she missed but as she seemed to date a man for only a short time, just long enough to enjoy the sex, having children seemed impossible. I never can seem to commit, thinks Gothia as she moves into the hallway.

As Gothia looks up to the third floor she knows she should unpack but the room on the third floor seems to draw her. As she unlocks the door, Gothia sees the room, as it was when she last saw it. Yet it was different in some way.

The scent of something old but not bad greets Gothia's nose as she moves farther into the room. It smells of Old Spice or maybe Bay Rum, scents her great grandfather and grandfather wore. These were smells Gothia remember from her happy days with her great grandfather and grandfather.

How weird, thinks Gothia as she moves over to the wardrobe.

This is being wasted up here, I need to move it to one of the bedrooms if not mine, thinks Gothia as she opens the drawer that held the picture.

The picture is still there but sticking out of another corner is what looks like another picture.

As Gothia pulls out the picture the same breeze she felt last time again blows across her cheek.

Ok, what is going on here, wonders Gothia as she looks at the picture. It is the same couple but this time they are in what is definitely wedding attire.

The groom is dressed in formal attire. The look on his face is a mixture of emotions it seems to Gothia. He looked happy yet there was another look in his eyes, one Gothia could not figure out.

The look on the young woman's face seemed to be one of utter happiness and yet also one of apprehension.

I still think the girl looks like me in some ways or I look like her thinks Gothia as she puts the picture back with the one that was already there.

As she moves over by the mirror Gothia glances into the mirror and then glances back again. For a second she sees a face behind her in the mirror, the face is that of a man.

Okay you are using your too active writer's imagination, thinks Gothia as she looks around the large room.

See no one is here; get a grip, thinks Gothia as she goes over to the door that leads to the small room.

This bed goes with dresser and the mirror, thinks Gothia as she sits on the bed. As she looks at the quilt, Gothia knows with a good airing this quilt would look good on this bed or hers.

The real estate agent had found an entire set of keys that she knew nothing about till they were going through the paper work on the house. With the set of keys was a small key that Gothia hoped was the key to the closet.

Okay, thinks Gothia, now I can see what they wanted hidden.

The key is small and looks like brass but fits the lock to the closet perfectly. After a little encouragement from Gothia the key turns in the lock. As she pulls on the closet door handle Gothia feels the breeze again, but this time it is as if some one or some thing had caressed her.

Some one or some thing is in this room with me, thinks Gothia. But, Gothia knows she is not afraid.

"Oh my Lord," gasps Gothia as she views the contents of the closet.

She expected to find something but the items in the closet were more than she expected.

Dress after dress hangs in the closet. As she gently lifts each dress, Gothia can see there are dresses for several occasions.

The first dress is pale blue and looked like it was more than casual, maybe what they called day wear for visitor, thinks Gothia. As she pulls out a rich burgundy colored gown, Gothia feels it was for formal occasion but not a ball gown. Its rich velvet material was a little worn but all in all it was a lovely dress. The next dress was definitely a church dress as it was gray and had a high collar and felt as it was made of light -weight wool.

The last two dresses takes Gothia's breathe away. A very formal dress made of satin and its color so deep blue it looks black and the last dress was definitely the wedding dress in the picture. It was slightly yellow with age but still lovely.

How could the previous tenants not find these dresses or why did the original owners not take them, wonders Gothia. The dresses were as old as the house.

As Gothia searches farther into the closet she finds two pair of shoes, more like the boots they wore in the early 1900's.

"Oh how cool," murmurs Gothia as she sits on the bed with the white pair in her hands.

They won't fit, thinks Gothia and is surprised as she slips them on to find them a perfect fit.

"Oh wow," murmurs Gothia as she stands in the shoes.

"Rebecca,"

"What," exclaims Gothia. "Who is calling me?"

Okay, now I am hearing things, thinks Gothia, but deep inside she knows she is not. But, she feels no fear.

Something seems to push Gothia back to closet. As Gothia peers into the closet she can see a box on top of the shelf. As she pulls it down Gothia sees another box behind this one so she pulls it down to.

The first box looks like an ordinary box until Gothia opens it. Inside is a very delicate and beautiful lace and silk negligee. Although it has a high collar the sleeves are sheer and the color is a delicate pink.

I want this; I hope it fits, thinks Gothia as she strokes the negligee.

"Rebecca," whispers the voice again.

"Okay who are you? What do you want?' asks Gothia. Although she feels no fear the hair on the back of her neck raises.

The other box looks like an old jewelry box. The wood is worn and the emblem on the lid looks like a family crest. The lock is a little rusty but as she wiggles it, it pops open.
Inside the box is what looks like numerous old newspaper clippings but also some several small jewel boxes.

"Rebecca you are here," whispers the voice again.

Gothia knows the voice is male.

"Yes I am here but who are you and how do you know my name?"

"Rebecca," says the voice again as a breeze glides across Gothia's face rippling her hair and then moving down her body slowly.

"Enough is enough," says Gothia as she takes off the shoes and puts on her own.

I'm tired thinks Gothia as she closes the closet but takes the negligee and the box with the clippings and jewelry with her.

As she moves downstairs she feels as if she is being watched, but she knows there is no one there.

CHAPTER V

Downstairs Gothia wanders from room to room.

The nightgown is hanging on a line in the back yard. The late afternoon sun warms it as the early Massachusetts fall breeze blows the negligee gently.

I will bring the dresses down when I bring the furniture down, thinks Gothia as she goes to her old New England Kitchen to prepare a cup of tea and a sandwich.

It is too early for her usual dinnertime but too late for lunch. Gothia knows she is hungry but as all her cookware and dishes are still packed a sandwich and tea will have to do. Her teakettle and cups are easy to find and as she had stopped at the store to get a few supplies a sandwich is quickly made.

Tomorrow I go shopping, thinks Gothia as she takes a bite of her turkey sandwich.

As she sips her hot, sweetened tea Gothia thinks over the voice she heard in the attic.

As she is a strong believer in spirits from the other side or ghosts as most people called them Gothia knew that the voice although real was not from this world or from some one living.

In writing her paranormal romance Gothia had done extensive research into the reasons for a spirit or ghost to still be here in the earthly world.

So what is your reason, wonders Gothia as she takes another bite of her sandwich. As she listens she waits for an answer but none comes.

"Okay so you don't want to talk," says Gothia as looks at the box beside on the table. As she opens the box Gothia notices a scent of lavender coming from the box, some thing she did not notice upstairs.

The newspapers clippings are old and yellow with age. As she lifts them from the box Gothia treats them tenderly so they will not fall apart.

One article talks about the building of this house. Stephen Edwards a wealthy banker had built the home for his new bride Rebecca. The house was one of the largest seen in this area and was reported to take over ten months to build with the workers working twelve hours a day.

The next article was a society piece reporting on the house warming party held in the home. For what she could tell the cream of society was at the party. The list of guest read as a who's who of the wealthiest in the town. Gothia reads on till she comes to the name James Smith and for some reason she feels something that could only be judged as fear.

As she lays this article down Gothia decides to look in the jewel boxes. The first box holds a string of pearls, very lovely and more than likely very expensive even for that time. The second box contains a cameo, delicate and lovely although the piece needed cleaning. The last piece is a locket heart - shaped; it is somewhat tarnished but cleanable. As she opens the locket Gothia sees the man woman whose pictures were in the attic. The woman has her black hair swept up and at the neck of her dress is the cameo.

"Who are you," whispers Gothia as she holds the locket in her hand. As she continues to hold it in her hand Gothia feels a breeze on her arm but it lingers and to Gothia it feels like her arm is being caressed.

Just as it feels as it is a kiss Gothia stands up.

"Okay, no way that is enough."

The feeling halts immediately but Gothia's skin tingles everywhere that it was touched.

"You don't know me well enough for that," laughs Gothia as she tries to quiet her pulse and racing heart.

"Well you are here and I am here and we have to work this out as I bought this house and I am not leaving," says Gothia as she sits her cup and sandwich plate in the sink.

As she moves to the living room Gothia sees Eric's painting sitting by the fireplace where she moved it o. The painting's dark, moody looks just add to the eerie feeling Gothia is having.

Sorry Eric, thinks Gothia as she turns the picture to the wall.

As there is not much to unpack in the living room, Gothia has it set up in a short while. The television is set up in a corner but looks out of place in the living room.

Gothia knows she watches very little television but invested in one for the news and the paranormal and science fiction movies she likes.

I'm tired, thinks Gothia, it must be late. But as she looks at her watch she sees it is only 9 pm.

"Okay I don't care," mutters Gothia, "I am going to take a bath and go to bed."

As she heads to the stairs Gothia remembers the negligee on the clothesline.

"Oh damn," mutters Gothia as she runs out to get the negligee.

The night sky is full of stars and Gothia feels a cool fall breeze on her skin.

As she turns to look at the small building at the back of the house, which now houses her small car, she looks up at the apartment over the garage.

For a brief second Gothia swears she can see the figure of two people in the window and it looks as if it is a man and a woman.

As she stares at the window Gothia feels as if the woman is reaching out to her for help, as it seems the woman's arms are being held by the man.

"Help me," calls out a voice and Gothia knows it is the woman's.

As Gothia moves toward the apartment something pulls on her.

"Not at night," whispers the voice.

Okay this is enough, thinks Gothia; you are losing your mind woman.

As she looks at the window the shapes are gone and the air seems clear and there are no more voices playing in her head.

Its bedtime but tomorrow I investigate, thinks Gothia as she looks up at the window where the man and woman had stood.

CHAPTER VI

As she runs her bath water Gothia is glad she had taken time to put sheets on her bed and unpack her clothes.

The master bedroom had its own bathroom with a large antique claw foot tub in it. A shower had been added as a modern convenience but tonight Gothia wanted a bath.

As the hot water fills the tub Gothia adds a drop of musk oil to the water. A candle is lit and with only her bedroom light on the bathroom is illuminated by the glow of the candle.

As she sinks to her shoulder in the warm bath oil scented water Gothia closes her eyes.

The voice from the apartment fills her mind, as does the voice in the house.

I should be afraid but I am not, but yet the voice in the house does not scare her nor does the woman's but the man behind the woman's leaves Gothia with a cold feeling. I need to find out what is going on here but I am not moving, thinks Gothia as the hot water eases her sore muscles and the scent of the oil her mind. It is not long before Gothia feels herself drifting off to sleep.

The room is full of people. The band in the corner is playing a waltz. Gothia twirls in a deep blue dress, the skirt swirls around her ankles. The pearls on her neck gleam in the lights of the chandelier.

Her partner holds her firmly but yet tenderly. The smell of Old Spice is on him. His moves are easy to follow and Gothia glides with him across the floor till they reach the door to the garden.

As he leads her out to the gardens Gothia can smell the wild roses that surround the house.

The man's arm around her makes Gothia feel safe.

As her partner leads her to the fountain the soft glow of the moonlight reflects on the water.

"Rebecca," says the man, "My sweet Rebecca."

As Gothia leans into the man see can see into the fountain and the face so like hers but yet not hers stares up at her.

"Rebecca I love you and want to ask you something," says the man as he holds Gothia closer."

As she waits for his question Gothia knows what it will be.

Just as the man is to speak another man comes out of the doors.

"Well there you are, it is time for our dance Rebecca," says the man as he moves toward Rebecca and her partner.

"Our dance," says Gothia as she looks at the man.

His look makes Gothia feel dirty and she moves closer to her partner.

"You don't mind do you Stephen," says the man as he takes Gothia's arm and moves back toward the house not waiting for an answer.

With a moan Gothia wakes, her bath water is getting cooler and suddenly it is not so relaxing.

Okay that was a dream but yet was it, wonders Gothia as she wraps a towel around her body.

As she stands in front of the mirror the steam from the bath has fogged up the mirror so Gothia takes her hand and wipes it clean.

The streak of white in her black hair stands out vividly. As she stands there Gothia can see something in the mirror beside her reflection.

At first it is a black blur then as she stares closer into the mirror Gothia can see that there is the presence of a man behind her. His face is handsome yet there seems to a haunted look in his eyes.

As she turns around Gothia sees no one there.

This is all happening too fast, thinks Gothia as she goes into her bedroom.

As she lifts the negligee from the bed Gothia's towel falls from her body. The negligee still smells a little musty but Gothia knows it is clean and feels nice as it slides down her body. As she puts the towel back in the bathroom Gothia stares around the bathroom.

The room is empty and Gothia does not feel the presence that was there earlier.

As she pulls the blanket down Gothia decides the air is not that cool yet so the fresh air sounds good.

The windows in her room face the back of the house. Gothia decides one window is enough so she opens the one closest to bed. The night air is cool but not cold and the breeze blows through the screen gently. The lace curtains sway in the breeze but do not block it.

As she curls up under the covers Gothia feels at home, she feels as if she has found her place.

CHAPTER VII

The morning sun is bright and the air smells fresh as Gothia stands at her bedroom window.

Still dressed in her negligee Gothia knows she needs to get dressed. Although it is only 7 am. Gothia knows she needs to get to work on her house.

The phone company was coming at nine to hook up her phone and Internet so Gothia hurriedly makes her bed and then dresses in a pair of jeans and a sloppy sweatshirt.

As she sips a cup of coffee Gothia makes out her shopping list. Besides groceries Gothia lists more cleaning supplies and plans a trip to the local library to do some research on her new home.

As she unpacks the items for her kitchen Gothia glances out the window. The garage and the apartment over it are in her direct view.

Now would be the time for a visit to the apartment over the garage, while it was light, thinks Gothia.

For some reason she wants to delay her visit to the rooms over the garage so Gothia finishes setting up her kitchen.

Before she knows it, the clock shows it is 9:15.

I wonder where the phone company is, wonders Gothia as she sets up the last of kitchen items.   As she never seemed to have time to cook her kitchen shelves look bare as does the pantry and refrigerator.

I will fix the refrigerator issue today, thinks Gothia as her doorbell sounds.

After Gothia shows the serviceman where she wants the phone lines and modem Gothia walks back to her kitchen.

As she sees it is only 9:30 and she knows she cannot leave her house till the serviceman is gone Gothia decides to explore the apartment out back.

The stairs that lead up to the apartment are narrow but sturdy. The banister needed some painting but the roof looked as in good of shape as that on the house.

As she unlocks the apartment door, Gothia takes a deep breath.

This is silly there is no reason to be afraid, thinks Gothia as she moves into the apartment.

The apartment is very basic and there are basically only three rooms. The previous owners had not done much to modernize or use the apartment judging by the amount of dust on the cabinets and windowsills

The kitchen is small and old fashioned. There is a refrigerator but it looked to be very old and Gothia wonders if it works. The sink is the old porcelain kind. The kitchen cabinets were made of dark wood and the handles looked to be brass. With some cleaning the cabinets would look very nice, thinks Gothia.

The largest room was what must have been the living room and bedroom. Windows on three sides surround the room.

The room smelled musty but yet as she stood in the center of the big room another smell came to Gothia. It was a mixture of paint and some thing else.

I swear I can smell lavender, thinks Gothia as she moves over to a window set that is set against one of the windows.

As she lifts the lid to the window seat Gothia can see paintings, most of them unframed. As she pulls out the paintings they resemble the ones she saw in the attic room. An amateur did them but they are good. The first two are paintings of fruit bowls and flowers, some thing most beginning artist start out with. Then the paintings begin to change. The next one is one of the main house but in its heyday. The rose garden is in bloom and in the middle of the yard sits a sundial.

This one is not bad, thinks Gothia as she sits it down on the floor.

The next painting is one of a man, it is done in charcoal and Gothia senses a lot of work. As she looks at the painting closer Gothia gets the feeling she knows the man.

Oh my lord, thinks Gothia, it is the man in the picture with the young woman, but more than that it is the man she saw in the bathroom mirror and in her dream.

As her hands shake Gothia sets the drawing down and picks up the next one. This picture of another man, yet it does not show the work or maybe love is the word that the other painting showed.

As she looks at the painting Gothia sees it is done in charcoal and as she looks at it closer it looks like the other man in her dream. The way the man stands shows how proud he is of his looks.

He sure is cocky think Gothia as she looks at the man's face. She has to admit he is good looking but some thing about him scares her. He has an almost evil look on his face.

As Gothia sets it down she sees there is one more picture. The picture looks like the girl in the pictures upstairs and some thing tells Gothia that it is a self-portrait.

The girl has done the picture in pastels this time. She is dressed in a pale pink dress and she is standing against a window. It looks like she is in this room, thinks Gothia, as she looks at the picture closer. She looks sad, thinks Gothia as she notices the girl is not smiling and her eyes seem to hold another emotion; if I did not know better I would swear she is afraid of some thing or some one.

"Help me," whispers a voice in Gothia's ear.

"Who, what," says Gothia as she twirls around.

The smell of lavender is even stronger and then Gothia smells some thing else. A very strong odor of old spice hits her nose. It is so strong it makes Gothia sneeze.

"Rebecca," says a man's voice. The man's voice is not that of the man in the house and Gothia feels suddenly very cold.

"Rebecca you are here, I have you," says the man as Gothia feels the cold even more.

"I am not who you want," says Gothia as she moves from the spot. Gothia's hands are shaking but she knows she cannot back down.

As she puts the paintings back in the window seat Gothia can feel her heart beating against her chest.

"Help me, please," says the female voice again. Its sound is mournful and seems to fill the room.

"How can I help you?"

"No one can help her, she is mine," says the voice.

"The diary, please find the diary," says the female voice as her voice fades away.

"Diary what diary?" asks Gothia out loud.

As Gothia waits for an answer the smell of lavender fades away but the smell of the man's cologne gets stronger.

The diary, her diary I guess, thinks Gothia.

As Gothia looks around the room she knows the diary is not here, but she looks again in the window seat even though she wants to run from the room.

A search through the kitchen cabinets proves fruitless, as all she finds is cobwebs and a tiny little house spider.

The house it must be in the house, thinks Gothia as she hears a horn blowing outside.

"Oh damn," mutters Gothia as she goes to leave the apartment she feels a pressure on her arm.

"Rebecca, you are Rebecca," says the man's voice.

"No I am not," says Gothia as she pulls her arm loose from the invisible pressure.

As she locks the door Gothia knows there is more to this house than she thought and the man in the house does not scare her and the woman well the woman she feels sorry for, but the man in the apartment scares her.

The serviceman is waiting for her in the driveway.

"Ma'am we are through and you have phone and net service now."

"Thank you fine," says Gothia as the truck pulls out of her drive.

I must find that diary, thinks Gothia as she moves back in the house. But first a trip to the store.

CHAPTER VIII

It has been two days now, thinks Gothia as she drinks her morning cup of coffee, and I still have not had the time to look for the diary.

First it was her publisher calling her about her writing. The publisher seemed more worried than Gothia that nothing was coming. But, she did have news for Gothia. It seemed that her latest novel had the attention of a TV station who was considering it for a made for TV movie. The publisher told her she would get back with her with more details when she got them.

Then it was a plumbing issue, there was a leak in the kitchen pipes and it took a whole day of dealing with a plumber to get it fixed.

The furniture from the attic had been moved to second largest bedroom along with the clothes and shoes she had found. Another box was found when the closet was emptied out but the box was locked and there was no key. Gothia searched the room in the attic but nothing was found that looked like a journal or diary. Maybe it was in the box she found locked.

Today I pick that lock, thinks Gothia as she plucks her toast from the toaster. As she puts her cup and plate in the sink Gothia looks out the kitchen window toward the apartment.

Some thing else she had not done was go back to the apartment.

The voice in the house had been conspicuously quiet but Gothia felt his presence in the attic when the furniture was moved out. The smell of men's cologne clung to the air and a gentle breeze blew her hair every so often.

I want to do some research on this house, thinks Gothia as she goes to her computer.

As she types in some key words a link to an old newspaper article appears on the screen. As she clicks on the link a smell reaches her but it is not of a man's cologne it is of lavender and Gothia knows the girl is in the room with her.

So you want me to read this, thinks Gothia as she begins to read the article.

"It is lies", whispers a voice, "it is wrong".

The article tells of the disappearance of Rebecca, wife of Stephen Edwards. The neighbors interviewed suspected that Rebecca was having an affair with Stephen's best friend James Smith.

"Lies, lies, it is not so", whispers the female voice again. The girl's tone is so sad and desperate that Gothia feels for the girl.

The article goes onto say that Mr. Edwards has offered a reward for any information that will help him find his wife and the mother of their young son.

"Where did you go? Were you having an affair?" whispers Gothia as she sees there are further articles related to the Edwards.

"Lies, it is lies," says the girl's voice again.

"Rebecca you left me but now you are back," says the man's voice and the smell of lavender leaves the room as suddenly as it appeared.

Gothia holds her breath as she hopes the girl will come back, but there is not a sound not even the voice of the man.

The article reports that Rebecca was never found and foul play was suspected as the police found a bloody rag in the studio behind the house.

Police at first suspected Stephen and did arrest him, but after further investigation it was ruled that there was no solid evidence to support so he was released. At the preliminary hearing James Smith was called as a witness for the prosecution not the defense.

That is weird I would think he would want to clear Stephen unless, thinks Gothia.

"Lies, lies," says the female voice again. "You believe the lies."

"No," says Gothia as she turns around. There is no one there or no one that can be seen but Gothia knows the girl is again in the room with her.

"He is evil," whispers the girl.

"Who Stephen?" asks Gothia as she feels the girls distress.

"No! Not Stephen. I loved Stephen, I love Stephen."

"Then who is evil?"

"The journal find my journal, oh god he is coming," says the girl as Gothia feels the room get suddenly very cold.

"I must go, find the journal, release me," says the girl as the sweet smell of lavender leaves to be replaced by the heavy, heavy scent of Bay Rum.

"Rebecca, yet not Rebecca," says a voice so cold that Gothia feels a real sense of fear.

"Leave my house," says a male voice. "Leave it now you traitor."

Gothia breathes a sigh of relief as the room begins to get warmer.

"You are safe Rebecca, my Rebecca," says the voice that some how Gothia now knows is Stephen.

"I am not your Rebecca," begins Gothia but she knows Stephen is gone.

As Gothia turns back to her computer screen her hands are shaking.

The rest of the article tells how at the hearing James Smith testifies how cruel Stephen was to Rebecca and that she was planning to leave him.

"Leave him for you, is what you thought," mutters Gothia as she reaches the end of the story.

So what happened to you Rebecca for Gothia knows the female spirit is that of Rebecca and the two men are Stephen and James.

Why are you three here, wonders Gothia as she looks for further information on the house.

Further tragedy seemed to follow the house as Gothia finds another old news story that tells how the bodies of Stephen Edwards and James Smith are found in the garden within a month of Rebecca's disappearance.

The final decision of the courts was that the two men got into an argument and from it seems shots were fired that proved deadly to them both.

God, no wonder the real estate agent did not want me to know the history of this house and no wonder it went so cheap and could not keep a tenant.

The young son of Rebecca and Stephen was sent to live with relatives and the house stood empty for years it seemed based on an article in a paranormal web site.

A deeper search into the history of the house showed that the house was purchased five years after the tragedy but was vacant with in a year of purchase. The couple that bought it was a young couple with a son. The wife reported noises and smells and her son saying he saw people in the house. The boy was four years old. The house stood empty for another two years and was bought by a young couple that turned it back to the bank.

A side note from the writer of the article said the woman felt afraid in the house. She reported noises and smells and the feeling of being watched. As she was pregnant she did not want to risk her baby's safety

At that time people just did not investigate haunted houses it seemed for no one came to investigate till the sixties

The house stayed empty for five more years and again was purchased. The owners left in the middle of the night it seems and left all their belongings.

The house then stood empty for over forty years. A couple then bought it with three children. The wife again was the reason the house was sold. She reported the same smells and noises but also reported seeing people in the house and in the apartment behind the house.

The couple sold after one year of residency and it stayed empty till the eighties where it was purchased as a bed and breakfast. This lasted for years and the bed and breakfast was listed as haunted by the most haunted sites in North America.

Well, it seems I should have done my research, thinks Gothia.

The bed and breakfast closed due to the poor health of the owners and stayed empty after that.

Till I came along, thinks Gothia as she turns off her computer. I must find that journal, thinks Gothia as she goes back to the kitchen.

It must be in the box, thinks Gothia as she looks to where she put the box. It's gone, the box is gone.

As Gothia searches the kitchen she can find no trace of the box.

So you moved it some how James Smith, thinks Gothia as she knows it must be him.

"Rebecca I am so sorry I know it was there, your journal was there," murmurs Gothia as she stares out at the apartment over the garage.

I bet its there, thinks Gothia. But as much as she wants to Gothia knows she is afraid to go out there.

I must go there, thinks Gothia as the ringing of the phone makes her jump.

"Hello," says Gothia as she tries to quiet her fast beating heart.

"Oh yes Ms. Wagner, you and your partner at the real estate agency were wondering how I like the house.

More than likely you are afraid I am going to sue you, thinks Gothia as she listens to the real estate agent prattle on.

"I am fine with the house and everything that goes on in it."

Gothia notices the real estate agent chooses to ignore this comment.

"What? The ancestor of the original owners wants to see the house? Why?"

As the real estate agent explains that the man is the great-great-great grandson of the original owner and has always wanted to see the home place.

"Home place?" questions Gothia. "I thought his family sold it or his relatives."

As Gothia listens she now knows why the family let the house go. The son of Rebecca and Stephen grew to be a young man and came to live in the house during one of its many vacancies. He came with his wife and son. After his wife began seeing things the man worried that she was going insane so he decided to sell the house and he made the stipulation that a blood relative of the family may never buy it.

Gothia listens to this story but some thing inside her tells her that this is not the true reason why a direct descendant of Rebecca and Stephen cannot live in the house.

"I still do not understand why he wants to see the house?"

The real estate agent goes onto explain that he has always been curious about the house and remembers the stories related to him by his father who got them from his father and he from his.

"I see, well I don't know," begins Gothia but stops as she hears a voice in the room.

"Let him come," whispers the female voice that Gothia knows is Rebecca.

"Okay fine, he may come but what is his name?"

"His name is Stephen after his great-great-great grandfather but I believe he spells it differently and thank you; he will be by tomorrow evening at noon." says the real estate as she hangs up.

"Tomorrow, wait—damn," mutters Gothia as she realizes the real estate agent has hung up.

The nerve of the guy he thinks he can just show up with less than a days notice. I would not be letting him do this if you had not told me to Rebecca, thinks Gothia as she looks around the kitchen then out to the apartment over the garage.

Okay now I am talking to ghosts for ghosts I do have, thinks Gothia. And I want this settle for you Rebecca and for me.

Now to look for that box, thinks Gothia as she moves to the library to begin her search.

CHAPTER IX

Damn it, thinks Gothia as she plops down on her sofa. Its five o'clock and I have not had lunch or find the box.

You hid it well James Smith for I know it was you, you asshole. thinks Gothia as she decides dinner is in order.

As she moves to the kitchen the fading light of the sun reflects in the window and Gothia knows she has waited to late to hunt for the box in the garage apartment.

It is not that late and you know it Gothia, there are lights in there, thins Gothia as she pulls out the fixings for a salad and the vegetable beef soup she made from the day before.

A drink would be nice but I will wait for later, I will need it thinks Gothia, as she knows she is going to the apartment over the garage. Waiting for daylight won't make it any easier.

As she eats her dinner Gothia thinks over the newspaper articles.

Two murders that were known about but Gothia knew in her heart that Rebecca did or would not leave her husband and son.

"I am so sorry Rebecca, I know you did not leave," murmurs Gothia as she puts her empty dishes in the sink.

"Okay here we go," mutters Gothia as she moves outside.

The apartment still smelled of musty air with a hint of paint.

Okay where did you put the book you sorry piece of dirt, thinks Gothia as she moves from cabinet to cabinet in the kitchen.

Nothing here, thinks Gothia as she moves over to the window seat.

"Help me, free me,' whispers the female voice.

"I want to free you, help you but free you from what and help you how?" asks Gothia as she stands by the window seat.

"The journal, please find the journal," says the voice of Rebecca.

As Gothia looks through the window seat a chill begins to fill the air around her. Is it getting colder in here, thinks Gothia, as she rubs her arms.

Then the smell of bay rum begins to fill the air.

Oh god, he is here but from where, where is he when not here, wonders Gothia as she moves as bravely as she can to the bathroom.

"Hurry, hurry it is getting dark, he is stronger at dark," says the voice of Rebecca.

As Gothia moves into the bathroom she looks around. There are not too many places to hide a box but Gothia opens the cabinet and finds it empty except for a bottle, the bottle is labeled bay rum.

"Rebecca for you are my Rebecca. I have you and her. For you are her reborn," says a voice so cruel, so cold that Gothia knows it is James Smith.

" I am not yours," shouts Gothia as she looks up at the bathroom mirror. There is more than just her face in it.

A man's face appears over her shoulder, handsome but utterly evil.

"I am not afraid of you," says Gothia even though she knows she is.

As Gothia moves away from the mirror she sees some thing sticking out from under the claw foot tub.

As she reaches down to pick it up, Gothia feels a pressure on her arm

"Let go now," says Gothia as she jerks away from the pressure but it remains and increases in strength.

"Let her go," says the voice of Rebecca. "You have me."

"I WANT YOU BOTH," screams the voice.

"No, I will set her free," screams Gothia as she grabs the box under the tub and runs out of the apartment.

As she moves back in the house, Gothia wonders if James Smith will follow her.

"He cannot hurt you here, here in this house, he came before not caring that Stephen was here but Stephen is stronger than him," says the voice of Rebecca.

"Why can't you talk to Stephen?" asks Gothia.

"He thinks I betrayed him, the journal will set me, set us free. I miss him, I want to join our son in Heaven please help," says the voice of Rebecca. "He killed m, I wouldn't have him so he ruined me, killed me, and took me away from my son and Stephen."

"He killed, you, then where is your body," asks Gothia. As she waits for an answer there is none.

She has left again, thinks Gothia.

As Gothia holds the box close to her she hopes and prays it is the means to free Stephen and Rebecca and to send James Smith to hell where he belongs.

CHAPTER X

As Gothia stretches out on her bed she feels better. The long, hot bath helped ease her body and her mind. There were no interruptions from Stephen or Rebecca.

It takes a little while but just as the clock clicks over to midnight Gothia find herself drifting off to sleep.

The roses smelled so sweet, their perfume filled the air. Rebecca leaned out the window to smell their fragrance better.

Today is my wedding day. Today I become Stephens' wife.

As Rebecca looks around she sees many of her friends and Stephens gathered in the garden.

There is my best friend Cecilia who will be my maid of honor and her husband John who is to be one of Stephen's ushers, but who are they talking to, wonders Rebecca as she leans out to see.

As Rebecca sees whom the man a shiver goes through her whole body and a feeling akin to fear grips her soul.

James Smith, to the world Stephen's best friend and his best man at the wedding but to Rebecca he is the devil incarnate.

When she first met James Rebecca had taken an instant dislike to him. His handshake seemed too familiar and the looks she caught him giving her were not those of a man who was her boyfriend's best- friend. Rebecca knew she tried hard to get along with and like him for Stephen's sake, but this seemed to lead James Smith to believe she liked him for himself.

His looks had become more lecherous and twice in the last two weeks he had maneuvered it so that she was alone with him; once in the library and once in the garden.

Luckily Stephen had come in the library before James Smith got too familiar. He had moved close to Rebecca and had put his hand on her arm, just as he was moving to close to her breast Stephen walked into the room so James dropped his hand quickly.

Stephen had quizzed her as to why she looked so pale and her excuse was she had very little to eat that day. She cringed when James Smith winked at her behind Stephen's back and mouthed good girl.

Out in the garden a week after the library episode James had caught her again alone, some thing Rebecca had tried to avoid at all costs.

James cornered her as she stood looking up at the studio apartment Stephen was building for her. As she loved to paint and was good at it he wanted to encourage her by giving her a space that was all her own.

James began his unwanted advances quickly by walking up to Rebecca and putting his hands on her shoulder. At first she thought it was Stephen but then James Smith begin to whisper in her ear and as Rebecca tried to pull loose, James Smith tightened his grip so that it hurt.

James began to whisper how he wanted her and that she was too much woman for Stephen.

He then began to tell her just what he would want from him if she were his wife. Rebecca struggled to pull loose but the painful grip became even more painful.

Just as she felt his lips on her neck James Smith pulled away quickly.

Stephen, Cecilia and John walked out to garden.

As Stephen walked up to her, Rebecca recalled his touch on her shoulder and how she cringed as it hurt.

Stephen did not notice her look, as it was dark.

John and Stephen teased James about being a bachelor and coming to their little party tonight with out an escort.

James just laughed and told Stephen that he was just hoping Rebecca would run away with him and it was lucky for John that Cecilia and he were married as he did not chase after married women.

Stephen laughed as he thought James was joking and he told him he was sure Rebecca was very happy with him.

Rebecca remembered holding on to Stephen's arm and telling him and the rest of the group how James was totally out of luck as Stephen was the only man for her.

This comment got her a kiss on the cheek from Stephen and a scowl from James Smith.

Stephen laughed and told her that James was dumbfounded as most women found him totally magnetic and alluring.

Rebecca told him she was a not most woman.

As Rebecca starts to move back into the bedroom to straighten her wind blown hair, James Smith looks up at her.

"Hello Rebecca, you look lovely," he calls up to her. "Too lovely for Stephen," he says with a laugh but Rebecca senses a threat in those words.

As she walks to the center of the bedroom that is to be hers and Stephens, Rebecca rubs her arms. It is not cold but yet she feels as if the cold predicts an imminent sense of danger.

As she shakes off this feeling Rebecca concentrates on her wedding and her love for Stephen.

The wedding ceremony is over and the reception is in full swing as Rebecca moves around to visit with her guests.

As she finishes talking to one of Stephen's older uncles, she feels hands on her shoulders and the voice turns her blood cold.

"Well, Rebecca so now you are Stephen's wife. You should have married me," says James Smith as he squeezes Rebecca's shoulders in what is more of a caress.

"Never and let go of me," says Rebecca as she pulls away from the man she hates more than any thing.

As people are staring Rebecca tries to compose her self, as Stephen is one of the people staring.

As she puts a fake smile on her face, James Smith laughs.

"I will have you Rebecca, don't you know Stephen and I share every thing."

As Gothia wakes, she knows deep inside that James Smith made good on his threat.

The clock light shows her it is four am. For some strange reason her shoulder aches, just as if it had been squeezed.

Okay I know you for the devil you are, thinks Gothia as she gets out of bed and walks over to the bedroom window.

There is no one in the window of the garage apartment.

"I will set you free Rebecca.   '

"Rebecca," whispers a voice.

"Stephen she loved you, loves you," says Gothia as she sees the reflection of the man she knows is Stephen in the window.

"You are Rebecca," says Stephen as Gothia once more feels his touch move on her skin, a touch she is no longer afraid of.

"I am not her, she is here and she loves you," says Gothia as Stephen touches her hair, her cheek and then her breasts.

She wants to tell him no, but some how his touch is familiar and so right. As he continues to caress her Gothia has flashes of memories. The memories of lying with a man in a bed are strong. The man is Stephen and Gothia feels the woman is she.

As Stephen's spirit becomes more familiar with her body, Gothia feels herself getting light headed.

The nightgown that belonged to the original Rebecca slowly moves off her shoulder and Gothia feels a kiss on her shoulder.

"No!" I am not your Rebecca."

The touch stops but Gothia knows Stephen is still with her. She can sense his hurt and confusion, as she feels confused herself.

"Stephen I am not your Rebecca, I am Rebecca but not her. She is here but you choose not to talk to her. I will help you, I want to."

As Gothia waits for a response she gets none and she knows Stephen is no longer in the room with her.

The clock clicks over to 4:30 and Gothia knows she needs sleep as she needs to be rested to help Stephen and Rebecca and energy to fight James Smith. She also knows that tomorrow the great grandson of Stephen and Rebecca will be here.

Lord, what will tomorrow bring, wonders Gothia as she lies back on the bed. Stephen's touch seems to still be on skin and Gothia feels a strong emotion almost like arousal.

"Okay time to quit this, he is a ghost and married so quit", says Gothia as she pulls the cover up to her chin and closes her eyes. "I am sorry Rebecca."

Just as she feels she will not get any sleep she hears a voice.

"It is fine you are me, and you will find out you are me."

I am she, thinks Gothia and she knows deep inside that this is true.

CHAPTER XI

The steaming coffee cup and bagel with cream cheese sit waiting for her as Gothia researches reincarnation.

Although one of her books had hinted at reincarnation it had been awhile so Gothia felt the need to refresh her self on the topic.

As she reads Gothia sips her coffee. It is hot and rich with cream, a luxury she can give herself, as weight was never an issue for her.

The bagel is crispy and the cream cheese so thick on it that it leaves some on her lip.

As Gothia wipes it off she feels a dip in the air.

"Okay who is here?" asks Gothia as she looks around the room."

"It is I," whispers a female voice.

"Rebecca," says Gothia as she strives to see the girl whose pictures she has only seen.

"I must hurry," says Rebecca.

"Where is James Smith?   "He is gone he wanders from the studio to the garden where he and Stephen fought," says the voice of Rebecca.

As Gothia stares toward the area the voice is coming from, a shape begins to form. Soon Gothia can see the shape of a young woman, it is gray in color but the face soon becomes clearer to Gothia.

"Rebecca I look like you but how?" asks Gothia as looks at the ghostly vision of Rebecca.

"You are me, I feel you in me," answers Rebecca as her shape fades in and out.

"I feel this too and I want to help you," says Gothia as for a brief second Rebecca's form becomes clearer and Gothia sees just how much she looks like Rebecca.

"Read the diary, my journal. It will help," says Rebecca as she once again fades away.

"I am this morning, oh damn that man is coming here," says Gothia as she recalls the ancestor of Stephen is visiting her today and soon.

"He must come, he will help," says Rebecca. "Oh I must go I sense James," says Rebecca as her voice fades and her appearance disappears.

"Wait, why must he come," asks Gothia as she looks around.

"Rebecca your name is Rebecca and my last name was Miller," says the ghost of Rebecca.

"Miller!" exclaims Gothia as she jumps up. "You are my ancestor."

As Gothia waits there is no answer and she knows that Rebecca has gone.

She must be my relative, thinks Gothia as she stands in the middle of the room that was once Rebecca's home and is now hers. As she thinks this over, a call to her father seems to be in order.

As she waits for him to answer Gothia takes one more sip of her cooling coffee. The bagel is long forgotten, as her appetite is gone.

"Hi dad, I am fine. How are you and mom?"

As Gothia listens to her dad she thinks over just what she can tell her dad. If she told him every thing she knows he and her mom will be in the car taking the five -hour trips to see her.   They worried about her even though they tried not to show it.

Her disastrous affair with Eric and her subsequent mourning of him gave them basis for their worry.

"Rebecca, are you there?" asks her father.

"Oh dad I am sorry, what was that last thing?"

"Oh you and mom are planning a vacation here to my new house," says Gothia.

I must get these ghosts out here soon, thinks Gothia as she wonders if they would appear to her parents. After all her father was a direct descendant of Rebecca's.

"That would be great dad. It has been a long time. But dad I need to asks you some thing but I cannot explain why I need to know not just yet dad."

Gothia can tell her dad is worried by the tone in his voice when he tells her okay asks away.

"What was the name of our relative who you said was murdered?"

"Why in the world are you asking that," asks Gothia's father as her mother listens in.

"Oh I am thinking of doing a book about a murder and it made me think of the story you told me," says Gothia as she crosses her fingers as she tells the lie.

"Let me think," says her father.

As Gothia waits for an answer she walks to the kitchen to fill her coffee cup.

"Okay honey, your mom helped me remember, it was Rebecca, Rebecca Miller. She was your   great –great-great aunt. I think she was my great-great grandmother's sister."

"Rebecca, but that is my name."

As her dad explains that it is just a coincidence, Gothia wonders if it was.

Her research has led her to believe that all things happen for a reason and fate can play a hand in many things.

I was named Rebecca for a reason just like I was lead to this house, thinks Gothia as dad finishes his reason for her being called Rebecca.

"Okay dad, thanks and I promise I will tell you the whole story soon, tell mom I love her."

As she hangs up the phone, Gothia knows she is her ancestor reborn, reborn to clear Rebecca's name and reunite her and Stephen.

For some reason Gothia feels the need to take a shower and change clothes before Stephen Edwards arrive.

I do not know why I want to impress him, my jeans and sweat shirt were fine, thinks Gothia as she puts on a dress, it is some what Victorian in its look with its lace around the collar but that is where the Victorian look stops as it is sleeveless and fits Gothia's body snugly.

As she stands in front of her bedroom mirror Gothia sprays her favorite perfume on her neck and arms.

This is crazy, why do I want to look nice for a complete stranger.

As she has an hour to kill before Stephen Edwards is to come Gothia decides it is time to look at the journal. The box is locked and her early morning was spent trying to pick the lock with out breaking it.

"Okay Rebecca you want me to read this, then help me get it open" mutters Gothia as she works on the lock once more.

As she wiggles the hair -pin once more in the lock, she hears a slight click.

Thanks, thinks Gothia as she lifts the lock.

Inside the box is a very old diary. It is covered in very old and worn blue velvet. As she opens the diary she sees an inscription.

To Rebecca on her 18th birthday, love Mother.

Wow her mother was my relative too, thinks Gothia as she turns the pages of the diary gently.

The diary began with details of Rebecca's eighteenth birthday party held by her parents. At the party were girls she had attended private school with. Also at the party were her relatives and boys she had grown up knowing. Boys her parents thought were from good parents and of wealth. Several her mother had hinted at would make good husbands.

The diary went onto say that getting married was not in her plans Rebecca wanted.

I want to paint, I want to go to Europe to travel and paint and live.

Gothia thought about the young girl who dreamed of being a painter and artist and wondered if she saw any of this dream realized.

The diary told about the music and food at the party. Dancing was planned for the party and one of the best orchestras in town was hired to play.

Several of the boys or young men had already asked her to dance. She promised them a spot on her dance card.

Gothia knew just by the words and how they were written that she had no romantic interest in these young men.

The next page told of how her cousin Timothy had shown up late as usual. Timothy one of her best friends and play mate as a young child. He and Cecilia and Cecilia's fiancé John had all grown up together.

With Timothy was a college friend of his he had asked to bring along.

As Rebecca stood there talking to John and Cecilia she saw Timothy come in and wave at her but her gaze was all for the man with him.

Stephen Edwards was tall, somewhat on the thin side but handsome. So handsome it took Rebecca's breath away.

Stephen stared at her in such a way it made Rebecca blush and duck her head.

Gothia smiled as read that Rebecca was used to the young men vying for her attention but this was different. This was a man.

He was the same age as Timothy 21, but he looked much older with his somber look except for the smile that seemed to be in his eyes when he looked at her.

Stephen walked over to me, the diary read, he took my hand and I felt a spark like I had never felt before when a man took my hand.

The rest of the party was spent talking to and listening to Stephen. His family was much more wealthy than hers it seemed as he had been to Europe twice once when he was eighteen and again just last month. He was a senior in college and planned to be an architect.

Rebecca forgot about her promises to dance with her friends when Stephen asked her not to dance with any one else.

When he left he asked her to take a ride with him tomorrow. He owned one of the vehicles called a motorwagen and it ran eight miles an hour he said.

Rebecca wrote how excited she was not, oh not because of the automobile but because of the man taking her in the automobile.

Just as Gothia turned the next page she feels a breeze against her skin and she knows she is not alone.

"You have my diary, you can help me," says the voice of Rebecca as the scent of lavender fills Gothia's nose.

"Yes I will try," says Gothia as she looks toward the voice of Rebecca.

"The diary is the answer," says Rebecca.

The room became quiet and Gothia thinks Rebecca has left till she hears the sound of sobbing.

"Oh Rebecca please do not cry, I will help."   "REBECCA," calls out a voice that Gothia knows is James Smith.

"Oh for this many years he has followed me and kept me prisoner, the diary is the only thing that will help me," says the voice of Rebecca between her sobs. "My body is here, he killed me here, one day when Stephen was gone with our son."

"Where, where did he kill you, where is your body?" asks Gothia but she gets no answer.   "You will be free I will help you for we are one," says Gothia as the scent of lavender leaves the room and Gothia swears she can hear Rebecca crying even though she knows she is not in the room with her.

As she turns back to the diary some thing inside her tells her to go look out at the apartment.

With the diary in her hand Gothia looks at the apartment and in the window she can see two shapes.

She sees the shape of a woman and a man. She knows they are Rebecca and James Smith.

Gothia feels a pressure on her throat and she knows that James Smith has his hands around Gothia's neck.

"Let her go now," screams Gothia as she rubs her neck.

"I will never let her go and you will not set her free, I made my bargain with the devil and I will have her forever, she will be forever thought of as a fallen woman," says James Smith as he pulls Rebecca back from the window, the young woman's ghostly arms outstretched toward Gothia in appeal.

"I will help her you sorry ass," says Gothia as she holds the diary close to her heart.

Just as Gothia goes to open the diary again the doorbell rings.

Well here he is, thinks Gothia as she goes to lay the diary down then changes her mind and takes it with her to answer the door.

As she opens the door Gothia gasps in surprise.

The man standing in front of her is the exact replica of Stephen Edwards, the ghost in her house. His clothes are modern as he is dressed in blue jeans that hug his muscular but slim body and he wears a light -weight sweater on top. His hair is dark and his eyes are just as dark.

"Are you okay," asks Steven as he wonders why the woman is staring at him.

She is pretty, thinks Steven, that streak of white in her hair is quite extraordinary.

"Oh I am sorry but you look like," begins Gothia.

"I look like my great-great-great grandfather," says Stephen as he peers over Gothia's shoulder into the house that was once his families. "May I come in?"

"I am sorry, yes of course," says Gothia as she blushes a little. You dummy, thinks Gothia as the man passes her to enter the house. He probably thinks you are an idiot.

"My name is Stephen Edwards," says Stephen as he puts out his hand.

As Gothia takes his hand a shock goes through her body.

Static electricity thinks Gothia as Stephen continues to hold her hand.

"My name is Rebecca," says Gothia. Why did I tell him my real name, wonders Gothia, as she likes the feel of Stephen's hand.

"Rebecca, that was my great-great-great grandmother's name," says Stephen, as the feel of Gothia's small hand in his larger ones feels so right.

I feel as if I have met this girl before, thinks Stephen as he stares at Gothia.

"Well Rebecca I am thankful you let me come to see the house. It has been on my mind a lot lately," says Stephen as Gothia pulls her hand from his.

"Well, Mr. Edward the real estate agent told me how important it was to you," says Gothia as she looks up at Stephen. Lord he is his grandfather all over, thinks Gothia as she looks at the man whose family was intertwined with hers.

"Stephen, please call me Stephen. Yes, it is but if I told you why you more than likely think you have a raving idiot in your home."

"I don't think you look like a raving idiot and believe nothing you tell me could shock me," says Gothia as she and Stephen move farther into the foyer.

"So this is the house where it all happened," says Stephen as he moves toward the library.

"What do you mean?" asks Gothia but she knows.

"The place where my great grandmother betrayed my grandfather, her family and where my grandfather was killed."

"Your grandmother did not betray your grandfather!"

'How would you know, I know what I was told," begins Stephen but the look in Gothia's eyes stops him.

"I just know," says Gothia as she thinks that she needs to hold back on what is going on in the house.

"That is not much of an answer," states Stephen, as he looks at the book Gothia now clutches to her chest.

She seems to think that book is important, as she has not put it down the whole time, thinks Stephen as he looks around the large library.

"This room is fantastic," says Stephen as he moves around the library. As he comes to the table with Gothia's books he stops.

"Oh you like this writer too, my ex loved her work. I think she has every book this woman has written."

"So what do you think of her?" asks Gothia as she holds her breath. Gothia had found that most men think very little of romance and many of the shied away from the paranormal. Good thing women do not, thinks Gothia as Stephen holds up one of her books.

"Well, I do not really read romance but she does have a good knowledge of the paranormal thing. She makes it believable."

"So are you saying you do not believe in the paranormal?" asks Gothia as she thinks, well he won't believe what is going on here then.

"No I am not saying that, and lately I think I might believe any thing," says Stephen as he lays the book back where it belongs.

"Well, maybe I should not tell you this but—" begins Gothia but the smell of men's cologne begins to gently fill the air and she knows Stephen, the original Stephen is in the room.

"What, what is it you should not tell me," asks Stephen as he looks around the room. The smell of men's cologne fill his nostrils but he knows it is not his as he is wearing musk not old spice as this is what it smells like.

Okay, he is not ready for you Stephen, thinks Gothia as she moves closer to Stephen.

"I am not sure if I should tell you but I am the writer of those book, I am Gothia. My legal name is Rebecca Miller." Oh shit, I did not mean to tell him my last name; maybe he does not know about Rebecca.

"Well, I am in the presence of a talented woman, and a pretty one," says Stephen as he wonders why he smells what he smells. Out of the corner of his eye he sees a shadow move across the room.

"So, Rebecca Miller is Gothia," continues Stephen, " I- wait a minute, Rebecca Miller?"

"Yes, that is my legal name," says Gothia and she knows by the look on his face that

Stephen is putting two and two together. Please no ghost right now, prays Gothia as she looks toward the corner of the room Stephen is glancing at and she to sees a shadow. Please not now, thinks Gothia.

As the shadow disappears Gothia breathes a sigh of relief.

"Rebecca Miller was the name of my great-great-great grandmother," says Stephen as he determines his imagination was playing tricks on him. The shadow and the smell were both gone and the woman in front of him had not acted as if she had seen or smelled any thing.

"Oh really well both are pretty common names," says Gothia as she cringes inside. Yes I am lying but if he feels that way towards his great-great-great grandmother how would he feel if he knew I was kin to her.

"Yes, I guess they are," says Stephen as he moves around the library, stopping at the corner where he saw the shadow.

Did he see something, wonders Gothia as she sees Stephen has stopped at the exact corner where Stephen 's ghost once stood.

"Well, I suppose you want to see the rest of the house," says Gothia as she points toward the living room.

"Yes please, this house has been on my mind a lot lately as I said before." On my mind and in my dreams, thinks Stephen as he follows Gothia to the living room.

Stephen cannot help but notice that Gothia has carried the book with her. What can be in that old book, for it is old that she feels the need to carry it with her everywhere, wonders Stephen as they move around the living room.

As Stephen stops in front of the painting over the fireplace he is struck by its despair and morbid atmosphere. I hope she is not the artist, thinks Stephen, its good but very depressing.

"A friend of mine did that some years back," says Gothia as she watches the look on Stephen's face.

"Your friend is good," says Stephen, as he knows that the friend was more than a friend by the look on Gothia's face.

"Was good," says Gothia as thinks about Eric. The loss still can bring an ache to her heart.

"Oh, I am sorry," says Stephen, as he knows the "was" comment meant her friend was dead.

"Thank you, he was very talented. I can show you the outside now if you want," offers Gothia as she hopes Stephen does not want to go upstairs.

"I was hoping to see the upstairs and then maybe the buildings out back," replies Stephen as he moves to the stairs that lead upstairs.

"Well," begins Gothia.

"I was told you were fine with me seeing the house and it is very important to me to see the rooms upstairs," says Stephen as he waits on the bottom step of the staircase.

"Let him go," whispers Rebecca into Gothia's ear.

"Okay it is fine," says Gothia as she moves past Stephen up the stairs. As she passes him her arms brushes his and Gothia feels a shock through her body.

Static electricity, thinks Gothia, but inside it is as if she knows this man. He seems to be the living replica of the original Stephen.

As they move into the hallway, Stephen seems to know his way around the house as he moves immediately to the master bedroom.

"This is the master bedroom," says Gothia as Stephen moves around the room.

"I know," replies Stephen as he stops at the window to look out toward the apartment out back.

"You know?" asks Gothia as she wonders about this man. Is he nuts or intuitive?

"I mean it figures as it is so big and has its own bathroom," answers Stephen. The girl is going to think I am nuts but I know this room for it has been in my dreams. In my dreams of a world long ago, making love to a woman. A woman who seems to be so much like this girl here that Stephen wonders if he is not a little nuts.

A movement in the window of the apartment outside catches his attention and Stephen stares closer.

I swear I see a woman in the window, thinks Stephen.

The look on Stephen's face tells Gothia that he has seen some thing and she wonders just what.

"Mr. Edwards are you okay?" asks Gothia as she moves to the window.

As she stares at the apartment outside Gothia sees nothing in the window but senses that there was something there for Stephen to see.

"Stephen, just Stephen. Mr. Edwards was my father," says Stephen as he looks at Gothia. The woman's figure had faded from the window. A woman Stephen sensed he knew.

"Well then Stephen are you okay?"

"Yes, I am but are you?"

"What do you mean? " I am fine," says Gothia as she feels herself clutching Rebecca's journal closer to her heart.

"Just this, why is that book so important to you? You clutch to you as if it is a matter of life and death."

"I have no idea what you are talking about," states Gothia but her release on the journal does not lighten.

"Okay, I guess it is none of my business," says Stephen as he moves to the hall.

"It is his business, he believes me to be bad, you must share my journal," whispers the voice of Rebecca.

"Not now, not yet, I need to read it alone," whispers Gothia.

"Did you say something Rebecca, I mean Gothia," says Stephen as he stares at Gothia.

"No nothing," says Gothia, " and you can call me Rebecca."

"I would like to see the attic room please," says Stephen as he moves to the narrow stairway that leads to the attic.

"How do you know about the attic?" asks Gothia as she moves with him up the stairs.

"I really cannot explain it and if I did you would think you were talking to a nut," says Stephen as they enter the large attic, empty of all the furniture it once held it seems barren and sad to Gothia.

"I promise you when it comes to this house nothing would seem weird."

"What does that mean Gothia I mean Rebecca," says Stephen as he looks around the room.

" I – well lets just say the house seems to hold many a story and a mystery," says Gothia as she opens the door to the room that once held the furniture now on the second floor.

"This house and its story has been a part of my life ever since I can remember," says Stephen as he moves around the small room and over to the closet.

"There were items in this room and the bigger room but I have moved them," says Gothia as she senses she and Stephen are not alone.

The smell of Old Spice drifts into her nose and a sense of something other than fear fills her body.

"You are here Stephen, aren't you? You wonder who this man is or do you know," whispers Gothia as she can feel the ghost of Stephen move from her side to that of his great –great-great grandson's.

"This is strange but I smell men's after shave and not mine, it is from some one else," says Stephen as Gothia watches the shadow of Stephen's ghost fade in and out.

"I think we need to get out of this room," says Gothia as she unconsciously takes Stephen's arm to lead him out of the room. She knows some how that Stephen is not ready to meet Stephen.

"Why, you seem to be hiding some thing from me," says Stephen as he resists Gothia's pull on his arm. " I need to know more of this house, I cannot explain why but I am tied to it and I cannot seem to let go."

"I too feel you are hiding something from me or not telling me the whole story," retorts Gothia as Stephen's attitude is beginning to irritate her to no end.

"Not really I assure you but if I told you what has been going on for several months you would think I was nuts and asks me to leave your house,' says Stephen as he feels some thing in the air.

I sense we are not alone, thinks Stephen as he looks around. The smell of a man's cologne not his again fills his nostrils.

A shape forms out of the corner of his eye and Stephen swears it is the man in his dreams, his great –great- great grandfather.

Okay am I going nuts, thinks Stephen as he watches the shape fade in and out or is this the man I have been dreaming of; the man who called me back to this house.

" Are you okay Stephen?" asks Gothia as she sees the look on Stephen's face. As Gothia looks toward where Stephen is looking she sees the ghost of Stephen standing there.

Does he see him also, wonders Gothia.

"You are right, we need to leave this room," says Stephen as he pulls Gothia out of the room.

Stephen moves down the stairs and walks outside to the porch. His heart is beating so fast he can almost see it through his clothes.

"Are you okay Stephen?" asks Gothia as she steps out on the porch with Stephen. She knows deep inside that he has seen some thing, whether or not he will admit it is another issue.

"I am fine but I need to see the room out back, it is something that must happen now."

"Excuse me but I although you are not telling me everything I am trying to be considerate of that fact that this was your ancestral home but you do not make demands," says Gothia as she feels Stephen's ghost behind her.

"He must go there, I know he is my grandson," whispers Stephen. The whisper feels like a breeze against Gothia's skin.

"Okay lets go back there but I really feel you owe me an explanation," says Gothia as she walks out toward the back of the house.

"I am grateful for this but as for sharing a story, I believe we both need to share don't we Gothia?" asks Stephen as he stops and stares at Gothia.

His eyes seem to look right into her soul and Gothia feels as if she has known this man, known him a very physical sense.

The very thought of this puts an unaccustomed blush to Gothia's cheeks making her even more attractive to Stephen.

"I have no idea what you are talking about and the only thing we possibly share is the fact that I now own your ancestral home," retorts Gothia hating the warmth she feels on her cheeks and also hating the fact that he is right. They share more than the house.

As they enter the room all seems quiet. There is no sense of cold or the usual smells that seem to accompany the room. This in itself strikes an odd feeling in Gothia. It is almost like the calm before the storm, she thinks as she watches Stephen move around the room.

As he walks over to the window seat he leans over it and opens it.

"These pictures are good, amateur but good," says Stephen as he pulls one after another out of the window seat.

"He is my blood, my grandson and he believes me evil," whispers Rebecca's ghost into Gothia's ear.

"It is all he heard, he does not know the truth no one does," answers Gothia out loud unconsciously.

"Did you say some thing," asks Stephen. As he looks toward Gothia he can see the shape of something beside her but it wavers in and out.

"No, I did not say anything," says Gothia as she feels a tear from Rebecca's eye touch her shoulder.

I feel her tears, thinks Gothia. I feel her pain.

"I know you said some thing but I do not think it was directed at me," says Stephen. "Gothia I need to know who were you talking to or thinking you were talking to."

"I was just talking to myself," lies Gothia as the ghost of Rebecca touches her shoulder. The touch should be cold but it seems warm and assuring. "I know I guess that makes me sound crazy."

"After my last few months experiences I assure you nothing sounds crazy but you were not talking to yourself," says Stephen as he walks over to Gothia.

"Gothia, he knows tell him," whispers Rebecca's ghost.

"Stephen, do you believe," begins Gothia but before she can say more a smell fills the room.

Oh god, thinks Gothia, James Smith is here.

Stephen can smell the man's cologne in the air and the room has seems to get colder. The shadow behind Gothia has faded out and another seems to hover behind her.

"What the hell is going on here?" asks Stephen as he sees the fear in Gothia's eyes.

"We need to leave this room now please," says Gothia as she feels James Smiths hands on her shoulders.

"You brought Stephen here but yet he is not Stephen," says James Smith as he squeezes Gothia's shoulders.

The pain is intense and Gothia winces in pain.

"What is wrong, what is going on?" asks Stephen as a sound like a man's voice enters his mind.

The voice is one from his dream, one of three.

"Please get out now!" exclaims Gothia as she tries to pull free from James Smith. His hands have now moved to her neck and Gothia can feel him squeezing the air from her body.

"Let her go James, let her go. I am here I won't leave. Please do not hurt her," whispers the ghost of Rebecca at the same time she pulls on his arm.

"I said I want you both," says James as he squeezes tighter on Gothia's neck.

Stephen watches, as Gothia seems to fade before his very eyes. He cannot see anyone but he knows she is being choked.

"Gothia/Rebecca!" exclaims Stephen as he rushes to save Gothia. Save her from what he has no idea.

"Stephen's grandson, your grandson Rebecca," says James Smith as he feels his grip on Gothia weaken. With Rebecca to help her and the presence of Stephen he had less control.

From out of nowhere a voice shouts, "Leave her alone you coward. You will not have her."

"Stephen oh my Stephen," says the ghosts of Rebecca as faces James Smith.

"He could not save me but he will save her," says Rebecca's ghost.

"No one can save you, you are mine forever," says James Smith as he pulls Rebecca to him and out of the room.

"I will save you Rebecca," whispers Gothia as she faints.

CHAPTER XII

As Gothia comes to she finds herself in her living room. Stephen is kneeling beside her with a glass of water in his hand and a worried look on his face.

"Rebecca are you okay? What in the hell happened out there?" asks Stephen as he sits beside Gothia and hands her the water.

"I- it was bad, he wanted to hurt me," says Gothia as she takes a sip of the cold water. Gothia knows James Smith meant her severe harm and the presence of Stephen and Rebecca's grandson made it worse.

"Who wanted to hurt you, we were not alone there were we; but I did not see any one," says Stephen as he recalls the past few moments.

"You did not see anything or choose to say that," says Gothia as she sits up. She knows Stephen saw what she saw but can he admit or does he believe it would be another story.

"What do you mean? Why through all this do you keep that book so close to you? You put in your pocket when we went to the room outside and now you have it in your hands?"

Gothia looks and unconsciously she has pulled out Rebecca's journal and now holds it close

" I think that more is going here than you will admit and more than I can even begin to understand," says Stephen as he walks back and forth across the room. For months now he had been having the same dream, a dream that seemed so real and evolving.

In the dream he was his great grandfather that was murdered but yet he wasn't. He saw everything through his grandfather's eyes but yet stayed himself.

"All I can say is this house holds secrets, tragedy, sadness and violence," says Gothia as she hesitates sharing all with this man she just met; but yet she felt like she knew him in every sense that a woman knows a man. This feeling had come to twice now and Gothia wonders why she knows him as she does.

"The only thing I do know is what I was told as a child by my father, and grandfather and that is that my grandmother cheated on my grandfather with another man and then left, leaving her husband and child and was never seen again. And that after finding out who the man was fought him and died in the back yard," says Stephen as he stops his pacing to look directly into Gothia's eyes.

"Just where did they get that story?" asks Gothia as she feels her temperature rising and the room's dropping.

"It was passed down as I said and basically gathered from newspaper clippings and stories from relatives of the past. I don't understand why you should care or why it is making you so angry as I can tell it is," says Stephen as he begins to notice a chill in the room. A chill that should not be as it is a warm day for fall.

"As a writer I have learned to believe half of what I read or hear," says Gothia as she debates whether to tell Stephen the truth about her connections with his family and the house that was once his families' home.

" I would tend to agree but as Rebecca disappeared and was never heard of or seen again would more than likely put credence to the stories passed down," says Stephen as he notices the chill of the room becoming more pronounced and what appears to be a man's from fades in and out quickly on the stairs. Stephen also notices that Gothia seems to be really pissed and wonders why a complete stranger would care about a woman who abandoned her family many years ago.

Gothia thought about this and the fact that she knew that the reason Rebecca left was not one of her choosing, but till she read more of the journal and till she found the body silence seemed to be the best idea.

"All I can say is that stories get twisted or changed as they are told over and over again," says Gothia as she watches the shadow of the original Stephen's ghosts fade in and out. Gothia felt as she could read his mood and it was one of confusion, angry and even some sadness.

"Stephen, Rebecca was not unfaithful and her body is here. I will find out the real story, I promise," whispers Gothia as she watches Stephen's spirit fade away completely.

"I have the feeling you were not talking to me," says Stephen, "but I won't asks who."

"I tend to speak my thought out loud that is all, I just think you need to leave an open mind to the idea that your grandmother may not have left voluntarily or at all," says Gothia as she wishes this man would leave so that she could read more of the journal. Also, his presence stirred up memories and feelings that made no sense. Memories of a life long ago happy and yet tragic.

"That is a very cryptic statement but I have the feeling you are not going to tell me what it means," says Stephen as he stares at Rebecca.

Whether Rebecca or Gothia she is a pretty girl, thinks Stephen as he gets the feeling that the girl would like him to leave.

"I really want to learn more, I want to know why this house was sold, why a family member could not buy it and if what you are saying is the truth and my great grandmother did not leave, then what happen to her. But I also get the idea you want me to leave and although is your home it is my family home, my past, do you understand this Rebecca?" asks Stephen as he moves closer to Gothia.

"Yes I do and I want to help you but it has been a hard couple of hours," begins Gothia. I too want to learn more as this is my family too, thinks Gothia.

"I know that well I will leave but I will be back, tomorrow," says Stephen as he moves even closer to Gothia.

"Yes tomorrow early if you want I can fix breakfast," says Gothia as the sense of knowing this man before fills her mind again. Memories of making love flash across her mind and the thought brings a blush to her face.

Stephen wonders at the blush to Gothia's cheeks but also knows it makes her even prettier to him. The urge to take her and kiss her more than once crosses his mind but he shakes it off for if he did what he wanted Gothia would ban him forever from this home and Stephen knew he needed to know the story of his family and now he wanted to know more of this woman standing so close to him that he can smell her fresh and earthy scent.

"Here is my cell phone number, feel free to call me if you need me," says Stephen as he hands the piece of paper to Gothia. Now why in the world did I say that, thinks Stephen. Something tells me I need to protect this girl but from what.

"I do not imagine I will need any thing tonight but some rest but thank you," says Gothia as she slips the piece of paper in to the journal.

"Well I will be here say at nine if that is okay?" asks Stephen as he takes Gothia's hand in his.

Stephen's touch sends a shiver through Gothia's body and she quickly inhales to try and calm the beating of heart.

"Yes that is fine, I will have the coffee going unless you prefer tea," says Gothia as she notices that Stephen has yet to release her hand.

"I know tea is a east coast thing but I prefer coffee," says Stephen as he finally releases Gothia's hand.

"Coffee then at nine," says Gothia as the feel of Stephen's skin lingers on hers.

"Good night then and call me if you need me,: says Stephen as he turns and walks toward his car.

"I will but I will be fine," says Gothia as she wonders why Stephen keeps on urging her to call him when he will be back in the morning.

As Stephen gets to his car he turns and looks back at the house. The porch light cast a shadow around Gothia but Stephen feels it is not just the light casting the shadow.

I hope you are right Gothia, I hope you will be fine, thinks Stephen as she starts his car and heads to his hotel.

As Gothia locks her front door the feeling that things are going to get very wild over takes her and she suddenly wishes morning was here already.

CHAPTER XII

As Gothia runs her bath water she takes a look out toward the garage apartment. There are no shadows at the window and all seems quiet.

Too quiet, thinks Gothia as she strips off her clothing.

For once Gothia finds her bath not as calming as it usually is. The feeling that she was being watched made her unusually nervous. The idea that Stephen may be watching her did not bother her but the idea that James Smith was made her feel very uneasy.

I know it should bother me that Stephen can see me but some how he feels familiar, it feels like we have been together forever, thinks Gothia as she slips on Rebecca's nightgown.

As Gothia looks at her clock she sees it is only 7 at night and the idea of dinner crosses her mind. I really want to read this journal, thinks Gothia as she picks up the journal but I am hungry. Some dinner was in order but there was no way Gothia was going to leave the journal unattended so she grabs a light robe and slips the journal in the pocket of the robe and then slips on the robe.

Downstairs dinner is a sandwich and a glass of milk.

As she takes a bite of her sandwich Gothia flips through the journal. The writing in the book is neat and yet very feminine. The pages seem to run smooth.

As she flips a page Gothia sees a definite change in the handwriting. What was once and neat is now somewhat sloppy, the handwriting slopes on some of the lines and in some places on Gothia sees spots where the ink has run.

I swear those spots look like tear drops. Thinks Gothia as she takes the last gulp of her milk and goes to get a second glass.

A certain page catches Gothia's attention.

He won't leave me alone, it begins, he follows me wherever I go. T*oday I was out shopping and*

I know he was following me. Twice I saw him behind me. But how can I tell Stephen, as far as he knows James is his friend and I am afraid of what he would do to James if he knew every thing James has done so far.

"What had he done so far?" whispers Gothia.

No sound comes from anywhere, the house is deadly quiet.

"Where are you Rebecca why don't you answer me?" asks Gothia as she looks around her kitchen.

There is no answer and in fact the room is quiet, deathly quiet, thinks Gothia. Damn, that was a poor choice of words, thinks Gothia as she places her plate and glass in the sink.

As she sits back at the table Gothia begins to read the journal again.

He is evil, it begins, *if he finds me alone he will hurt me.*

Stephen and I are so happy I am to have a baby, I just found out today. He is telling everyone. He wants to have a dinner party tonight. I know he will want to invite James, how do I tell him I do not want him here.

"Just tell him, well that was a dumb statement Gothia as this has already happened," mutters Gothia as she turns the page of the journal.

The dinner party is over; Stephen gave me a dozen red roses and a diamond brooch. His love and attention are wonderful and the night would have been wonderful if not for what happen later. Oh just writing it down makes me sick, but I must tell some one so I tell you my best friend. For in this journal can I write what ever want and know the only to see it is I for I will again hide it in my studio.

Stephen was telling the guest goodbye, everyone had left even our parents. The only one left was James Smith and his date. She seemed like a nice girl so I wondered why she was with him. I was alone in the garden. We had taken everyone out there to show them the flower gardens. The girl, her name Elizabeth had excused herself to freshen up. As I sat there I was so happy, a baby mine and Stephen's would be here in xix months. I did not hear him walk up behind me till his hands were on my shoulders.

At his first touch I knew it was not Stephen, his touch so cold, so cruel. His fingers squeezed my shoulder and the pain was more emotional than physical.

I told him to let me go and he just laughed. But his laugh was not one of joy.

He told me the baby I was carrying should be his.

I told him never. I told him I hated him and I wanted to stay away from me and my baby when it was born. I went on to tell him that I knew he had been following me and if it did not stop I would tell Stephen.

He squeezed my shoulder tighter and told me that this would only cause problems between he and Stephen and they had been friends forever. I would be asking Stephen to choose between him and me and was I that sure he would choose me.

I knew then that all of this would only hurt Stephen so I vowed I would avoid James Smith as much as possible and especially never be alone with him.

His next words sent a chill to my heart. I cannot have you as I want you Rebecca but after the baby is born I will have you and then before I could stop him he pulled me to him and kissed me. Oh yes dear diary I fought him, I pounded him with my fists but he was so strong. I really believe he would have done more if not for the fact of the baby and that he heard Stephen coming.

My poor Stephen wondered at my pale looks but I just told him I was tired. Oh how I hate lying to him.

Oh poor Rebecca, thinks Gothia as she continues to read the journal.

The next few entries talk about how happy Rebecca was over the baby but it also talked about how tiring it was to try and avoid James Smith.

At such a happy time the idea that James Smith was stalking Rebecca made Gothia angry.

" I will prove you to be the devil that you are James Smith and I will send your soul to hell where it belongs," says Gothia as she leaves the kitchen to go to her bedroom. She knows sleep is out of the question as she feels she must finish the journal to help Rebecca.

As she climbs under her covers Gothia sees it is now only 9 o'clock.

The house is quiet and the sense that she is all alone is puzzling to her. She cannot feel either Stephen's or Rebecca's presence and is grateful she cannot feel James Smith's.

The baby is born and we have called him Stephen after his father. Stephen filled my room with roses, dozen and dozens of red roses but the nurse he hired has made him remove all but one dozen from the room as she fussed that they were stealing the air from the baby and me.

My son is handsome, he looks like his father. I want him by me all the time as does Stephen.

Stephen is going to have travel for his architect company, I hate being apart from him but he says it will only be a few days at a time and he is also encouraging me to start painting again.

Gothia closes her eyes for a few seconds, the quiet of the house inviting her to sleep.

Just as she feels herself drifting off Gothia jerks herself awake.

No, I am going to read this journal, I am going to find out what happen and I will find where he buried Rebecca. Then she and Stephen can join their son and James Smith can rot in Hell.

The journal tells the story of a young mother and the joy she is experiencing with her son and her husband. It also tells of the relentless pursuit of Rebecca by James Smith.

This man's obsession with me haunts my life and if I would let it ruin my happiness with my son and husband, but I will not let it. He still comes to the house and has tried to find me alone at numerous times but I just tell the staff to tell him I am not in or indisposed. My maid tells me how he argued on several occasions that he must see me but they are loyal to me and make him leave. I believe my maid knows as does the nanny that he is no good.

Entries in the journal begin to be sporadic and Gothia sees the entries are some times twice but usually only once a week.

Stephen Junior is now 8 months old and I am back to painting. I hate leaving him for even an hour but I know he needs more than his mother.

The next few pages of the journal are some rough sketches. Good although small. The first one is of the baby.

Rebecca was right he was a gorgeous baby He had both the look of Rebecca and Stephen. This was what the current Stephen must have looked like as a baby, thinks Gothia as she looks at the next sketch.

This sketch is of Stephen and he is standing in the garden. The next is dark and brooding. The sketch is of the night and a woman stands in a room and behind her looms what looks like the shadow of a man with his arms stretched toward her.

"Oh this is a nightmare, but it was real," whispers Gothia.

The next entry is a written one and it details an event so horrendous it makes Gothia physically ill.

Oh dear friend I have been shamed, I have been abused. He found me alone and now I am so dirty. Stephen oh my Stephen when you return from your trip how can I let you touch me, I can't. Oh what can I do?

The studio so quiet and peaceful is no longer a place of solitude and creativity for me.

I have taken several baths but yet I cannot get his scent of me. I have sent Stephen Junior and his nanny to Stephen's mothers. I used the escape of a bad headache and she is glad to have time with her grandson. My mother called to check on me after talking to Stephen's mother, and I am very thankful it is their time at the shore. I told her I just needed rest but I need more.

How could I let it happen, I knew he knew that Stephen was out of town and would be for a week but I wanted to finish the portrait of Stephen for him as a coming home gift? The nanny had put the baby down and had retired for the evening to her room. I had let my maid Nancy off for the night and the rest of the staff were in their rooms. I sat there painting when I heard the door open.

I thought it was the nanny so I turned. There he stood in the doorway, a smile on his face. A look in his eye that told me I was trapped

I told him to get out but he just laughed. He told me that he had waited as long as he could. He said he knew Stephen was gone and the house was asleep.

I tried to push past him but he blocked my way, he put his hands on me and begins to kiss me, I tried to scream but he put his hand over my mouth. He begins pawing at my dress, I fought him but he was so strong.

After it was over he threw undergarments at me and told me to get dressed. He told me if I told any one he would hurt my son and Stephen.

As he was leaving he tuned and looked and me and told me we would do this again and a lot.

Oh I want to die what can I do, I am lost. I do not want to leave my husband and son but he will do this again, I know he will and I have no way to stop him.

Yes you did you should have told and let Stephen take care of it. This thought was unfair to Rebecca as back then women who stated rape were looked on as asking for it; wrong or right that is how it was.

As Gothia holds the journal to her chest she feels a sense of being very tired coming over her.

I cannot go to sleep, but sleep overtakes her just as if she had taken a sleeping pill.

Gothia feels as is she is floating. She can feel herself moving but yet it's not her. As she looks in the mirror she can see that she is Rebecca, her clothes are of that time, her hair is dark and piled high on her head.

She can see she is in the garden. The roses are in full bloom and the spot where the fountain she had been asking Stephen for had been started; the earth had been torn up and the shovels belonging to workmen still lay by where they had pulled up bushes. The stones for the foundation of the fountain lay in a neat pile.

Mrs. Edward," says a voice behind Gothia who knows she is Rebecca or seeing what Rebecca saw and feels.

"What, oh Nanny Grace, I am sorry is anything wrong?"

"No ma'am I just wanted to tell you that Stephen Jr. is asleep and I am retiring to my room."

"That is fine, thank you," says Rebecca as she looks at the nanny.

"Mrs. Edwards, may I ask you something?"

"Of course what is it?" asks Rebecca.

"Is there some thing wrong, I mean I know you are missing Mr. Edwards but the last four days you have seemed different. He will be home in a few days."

Rebecca looked at her son's Nanny but also some one she liked. To Rebecca none of them were servants but friends. I wish I could tell you Nanny Grace but how can I tell you that James Smith has now raped me three times.

"Nothing is wrong Grace, I am just missing Stephen, Mr. Edwards," says Rebecca as she sees a look of relief on the nanny's face.

"Good, then I will say good night, you will be coming in soon I hope," says Nanny.

"Mrs. Edwards, will be in shortly," says James Smith.

It seemed that James Smith appeared out of nowhere to Grace.

I do not like this man, thinks Grace, and I do not think Mrs. Edwards does either. He frightens me and I think he does her too.

"I can stay and uh fix you a drink or some thing," says Grace trying to stay as she can tell by the look on Mrs. Edwards face that she is upset.

"No, Grace you can go in," says James Smith as he puts his hand on Rebecca's elbow.

"I take my orders from Mrs. Edwards," blurts out Grace. The look on James Smith tells her is angry at her remark.

"Tell you servant not to be so insulting to me Rebecca," says James Smith as she squeezes Rebecca's elbow in warning.

"She is not a servant but staff and no Grace we do not need any thing I am sure Mr. Smith will not be here that long," says Rebecca. Oh Stephen I need you, thinks Rebecca as James Smith rubs his finger on her arm.

"Well, goodnight ma'am," says Grace as she turns and goes in.

Maybe I am wrong, maybe she does not mind having him around, thinks Grace as she goes in to check on Stephen Junior, but I hope I am wrong.

"Rebecca I get the idea you were trying to keep her here, you know that was not good, now come on," says James Smith as he pulls Rebecca toward the studio.

"Please no more, please," begs Rebecca as she raises her voice.

"Keep your voice down Rebecca, you know what I will do to Stephen and that son of his," hisses James as he pulls Rebecca into the studio

As Rebecca scrubs her skin, she can see the beginnings of a bruise on her breast. James Smith was harsh and more perverted this time.

If not for my son and Stephen I would die, oh Stephen how can I hide this from you.

I cannot tell him no and if I do I am fearful he will hurt worse or me my son and husband.

As Gothia wakes she knows she has again been Rebecca. Her skin feels as if it has been scrubbed raw from the washing and worse it hurts from the touch of James Smith.

Oh Rebecca, I hurt for you. He did you so wrong but if you were letting him have you to save your family why did he kill you?

The journal will tell me, thinks Gothia as opens the journal once more.

The next entry tells of Stephens return home. Rebecca's joy of seeing him is overshadowed by the guilt she feels and the fear she has for her life with him and her son.

Stephen senses a difference in me, he asks me what is wrong and I cannot tell him. He wanted to make love that first night but I put him off telling it was my woman time. Oh how I hate lying to him.

James Smith came over the next night after Stephen's return. He acted like he owned the house and was very obnoxious to Stephen. Stephen asked if he had been drinking. James told him no. He then begins to tell Stephen how he was over the house a lot and when Stephen looked at me I just wanted to run from room. James played it off as checking on his best friend's wife and son. Oh how I hate that man.

Stephen and I had our first argument. I told him I wish he would not allow James Smith to come here. I wanted to know why; I told him I just did not like him. He said that was no reason.

What do I tell him, your friend is raping me, and he has threatened to hurt you and our son. Oh dear journal what do I do.

Tell him, tell him but I know you did not, thinks Gothia as she looks out toward the garage. Once again the feeling that the house is too quiet

Gothia looks at her clock and sees it one in the morning.

I must have slept for a little while. but now I see it through your eyes Rebecca.

As Gothia watches, the pages of the journal open as if moved by a breeze, a breeze that could not be possible as the window is not open.

Stephen Junior will be a year old in a week. A year of joy and yet not. Stephen and I rarely make love now without the abuse of James Smith spoiling the moments. He does not understand, poor Stephen oh my poor Stephen.

I think he wonders about the relationship between James Smith and me. I see him watching James and me when ever that devil comes to the house. I believe he thinks there is some thing going on. Oh dear Stephen there is but not what you think or I believe you think.

Stephen is yet on another business trip. The day after he left which was three days ago I received a telegram from him. He feels there is some thing wrong or something going on, he has been talking to the staff and he wonders at the many visits by James Smith. He knows he has had to leave me alone a lot since the baby has been born but he loves me and could not handle the idea that I am unhappy or worse unfaithful. Oh my love I am not, but I must protect you and our son for I feel James Smith would harm you both.

The journal is spotted with smeared ink, which indicates to Gothia many tears were shed.

CHAPTER XIII

Sleep clouds Gothia's eyes once more, even as she tries to fight it.

The sounds of arguing fill Gothia's mind and for a brief second she believes she is dreaming.

As she sits up Gothia knows she has been woken up from an unsettled sleep by the sound of real arguing.

The voices seem to fill the room but there is no one in the room.

As she moves from the bed the voices draw her to the window. The building across her way is barely visible through the clouds but there is enough light to show the window of the apartment over the garage.

Gothia can see the figure of a man and a woman and by the actions she knows it is James Smith and Rebecca.

"You will not harm her," says the voice of Rebecca.

"I will not let any one else have her, I saw the look that grandson of your gave and she him," screams James Smith.

"My grandson, my handsome grandson, so much likes my Stephen," whispers Rebecca.

"Stephen, Stephen after all these years. Don't you realize you are lost to him forever and as for your grandson he believes you left him for me and believes you to be an adulteress," yells James Smith as his shadow seems to cover the whole window.

"He does now but with my niece's help he will realize that you killed me," says Rebecca, as her voice seems to get stronger.

"I have waited too long. Tonight I will take what is mine," says James Smith.

Gothia wonders as the voices quit suddenly.

Where has he gone, she asks herself as she strains to see the shapes in the window across the way.

Within seconds a chill begins to fill the air and Gothia knows that James Smith is in the room.

"I am not afraid of you James Smith, you are a rapist and a murderer," says Gothia as she pulls her nightgown to her; the nightgown that once covered Rebecca's body.

As Gothia watches a mist begins to forms and James Smith becomes more than just a shadow.

He is dressed in the clothes of the early 1900's. Although his features are not clear Gothia can see that he is handsome but in a very wicked manner.

"I have come to claim my prize," says James Smith as he moves closer to Gothia.

Even though she does not want to Gothia feels fear, a fear that grips her heart. I must run, thinks Gothia as James Smith moves closer to her.

If I do not escape he plans me harm, thinks Gothia as she moves slowly off the bed.

"You cannot escape me for I am stronger, I sense your fear and it excites me," says James Smith, as his form seems to become more solid, more threatening

I need to escape now, thinks Gothia as she moves toward the edge of the bed closest to the door.

"No leaving my dear," says James Smith as he moves in front of bed. His look is one of poor evil and lust.

"I am not afraid of you," screams Gothia although she knows this is a lie. "You are but a spirit, yes a spirit of evil but a spirit and no spirit can do me harm."

"You are so wrong my dear for you see I made a pact, a pact with my master," says James Smith with a sneer.

"Your master? Oh my God you mean the devil!" says Gothia.

"The devil," says Rebecca's spirit with a gasp.

"You stupid people may call him that we call him Lord Lucifer. I was tired of not getting what I wanted, I wanted power and riches and control of others.

"So that is how you made your money, how you could do people like you did and feel remorse," says Rebecca's spirit as her form became clearer to see.

"Remorse is for the stupid such as you and your stupid husband," laughs James Smith as he moves closer and closer to Gothia. "I plan to feel her and use her as I used you."

"NO!" screams Rebecca. "Stephen I know you choose not to know I am here, you believe what he told you but this girl is innocent and my relation, please help her," cries Rebecca as she tries fruitlessly to pull James Smith back from Gothia.

Just as Gothia feels the worse is going to happen a mist begins to form in the room by the bedroom door.

Slowly the form that Gothia had come to know as Stephen begins to materialize.

"You in my house, never," says Stephen as he becomes fully visible to Gothia's site or as visible as a spirits can be visible.

He is handsome and his bearing strong and determined.

"So Stephen comes to rescue the fair mortal, too bad you could not save your wife," laughs James Smith.

His laugh is demonic that Gothia shivers. Deep inside she prays for rescue but wonders if Stephen has the power to overcome such evil.

"What do you mean save my wife?" asks Stephen as his form moves between Gothia and James Smith.

"He means he raped her and then when she was going to tell you he murdered her," screams Gothia. "He raped her over and over and threatened to kill you and your son if she told."

"You lying bitch," yells James Smith as he moves or tries to move around Stephen. "Your wife came to me willingly and I was the one who broke it off."

"He is lying Stephen I loved you then, I love you now," cries Rebecca as she moves away from James Smith toward Gothia. "I was afraid, afraid for you and our son."

:I hear Rebecca's voice, why is it in this house, she left it so many years ago," says Stephen as he looks toward Gothia and the shape that is forming beside her.

"No Stephen, I found her diary with her help and it tells all," says Gothia. "James Smith used and killed and she kept quiet as she said to save you and your baby but it did no good as he killed you anyway and left your child with out either parent."

"That damn diary, you found it," screams James Smith. "Not without this bitches help," continues James Smith, as the air around him seems to get darker and heavier.

"Yes I helped her for after all these years fate brought her here and I knew she save me, and reunite me with Stephen and we could move on," says Rebecca. "Oh Stephen do you believe me, please say you do."

"I am so confused, you were gone, he said you were his lover and left to wait for him. I talked to people they said he was here all the time; you'd leave our baby to go with him. Rebecca, Rebecca I did you so wrong," cries out Stephen as he tries to move toward the spirit of Rebecca.

"No! I gave up too much to have her, I still have her and now I will have this one," screams James Smith.

"You gave what, you gave nothing, you took," says Stephen his whole body seeming to shake.

"I gave up my soul, I made a pact, and I was cheated. I was not suppose to die, you were along with her," says James Smith as he grabs Rebecca and drags her toward Gothia.

"I will destroy you Stephen and I will have your wife for eternity and this girl too," says James Smith as he begins to chant.

"No, he is reciting demonology," says Gothia as she tries to run from the room but it seems as if her feet are bound to the floor.

As James Smith's chants grow louder the air seems to fill with electricity and Gothia feels her legs get heavier and heavier.

"Pray Gothia, pray," cries Rebecca as she begins to pray out loud.

As Gothia begins to pray with her she can see James Smith getting angrier and angrier.

"NO! I am too strong; you cannot defeat me with your pathetic prayers. The girl is mine.

Gothia cringes as she feels invisible fingers move over her body. First they touch her face, her neck and then her breast. Gothia looks toward Stephen and then Rebecca for help but they seemed bound to their spot just as her. Gothia can see Rebecca's is crying but no sound comes from her lips. It is as if some one or something has bound her mouth, thinks Gothia as the fingers move to rip her gown from breast exposing them to all in the room. It is then that she realizes the fingers are those of James Smith as he is right next to her.

"Oh so lovely, murmurs James Smith as he places his spirit but yet weirdly physical hand on her breast. "I want to see more of this body,"

As he pulls her gown lower Gothia knows she is lost unless her prayers are answered. James Smith hand is now at her navel and pulling gown down lower. Soon Gothia knows her whole body will be exposed to his evil glance and touch.

"Oh dear Lord," help me," cries Gothia as she tries to pull loose from the spot she is bound to, but nothing happens.

"Love is the only thing that can save you Gothia," says Stephen. We love you, you have given me Rebecca back but now I am lost to save you, I am tied to this spot, as you are yours. Rebecca I love you and I ask your forgiveness."

"Oh Stephen," answers Rebecca as she feels the hand over mouth torn loose. "I love you and I forgive you, you could not know, it looked so bad."

"Shut up now," says James Smith. "I will not let you win." With this statement his chants grow louder and more profane.

"Oh please some one help us," cries Gothia as she also continues to pray.

"Gothia, Gothia," cries a voice.

"Stephen is that you, Stephen help me," cries Gothia as she hears steps run up the stairs.

"Our grandson Stephen, our grandson," whispers Rebecca as Stephen crashes into the room.

"What in the world<" yells Stephen as he watches the scene before him. Gothia is nude to the waist and before stand a man, yet not a man, as his form is somewhat wavering and see through. Also around Gothia are two other shapes and Stephen some how knows it is his great grand parents.

The figure in front of Gothia emits pure evil and his chant is one of demonic invocations.

"Move Gothia, move," yells Stephen.

"I can't, he has control," answers Gothia as she does try to move; her upper body is mobile but her legs feel like lead and will not move. James Smith's hand is moving down to rip the rest of gown from her.

"He only has control if you let him, let her go you bastard," says Stephen as he moves to Gothia. An electric shock seems to hit him as he grabs Gothia's arm.

"We must help him Stephen, we must help our grandson and my niece," cries Rebecca as her spirit moves to the side of her husband.

"No one can help," says James Smith as he continues his chant but Gothia can tell he is not as confident. She then realizes his power was in the fact that Stephen felt Rebecca cheated on him left him and their son and no longer loved him. Now that Stephen knew this to be untrue James Smith power was diminishing over Rebecca.

"Rebecca tell Stephen you love him, Stephen tell Rebecca you love her that is his hold on you and this house>" cries Gothia. "His power is gone if you still love each other."

"I love you Stephen, as God as my witness I never quit," says Rebecca as she tries to hold Stephen's hand.

"I know now my love and I am sorry for all these years I believed this evil man," says Stephen as he takes Rebecca's hand. "Go to hell where you belong James Smith, I love Rebecca and she me and we will finally be together."

As Stephen and Rebecca declare their love James Smith's demeanor changes. Gothia can see a glimpse of what appears to be fear cross his evil face.

"I may have lost you or so you think but I still have this girl," screams James Smith as he rips Gothia's gown off her. Gothia now stands naked in front of not only James Smith but also the spirits of Stephen and Rebecca and the ever present, warm –blooded, living Stephen. And Gothia feels shame more than fear now.

"Your love may free you and it may not but who will free this girl," says James Smith as he rubs his hand over Gothia's body.

The urge to vomit is strong but now Gothia knows she cannot show fear.

"I will free her, I am not afraid of you," says Stephen as he grabs Gothia's arm. I love this girl and I will make her my wife."

As Gothia hears these words she knows they are just words to save her but they feels so right as from the first moment she met Stephen she knows they were meant to be one. If there was a thing as reincarnation she and Stephen were the exact reincarnation of the two spirits now in the room with them.

"no, I cannot lose them both," shouts James Smith but his chanting begins and a look of fear crosses his face.

As Gothia feels her feet loosen she moves away from James Smith and pulls her bed covers around her. The room seems to pulse with a new energy and a white light seems to feel the room.

"No! no ," exclaims James Smith as his shape seems to quiver and fade. "I served him, he owes me, I am his, and he owes me."

As Stephen moves over to Gothia and puts his arm around her they watch together as the monster that was James Smith begin to fade even more.

"No, no this cannot be," screams James Smith as hands come from nowhere and pull him down as pulling him into the floor.

"Burn in hell James Smith," whispers Stephen as he tightens his hold on Gothia.

"Is he gone, is it over?" asks Gothia as she shakes violently. "Where did he go?"

"Don't you know," says the spirit of Rebecca. "He lost his hold on me and this house when my Stephen and yours proclaimed their love for us. He has been sent to Hell to serve his master."

"Then this over and you are free Rebecca," says Gothia.

"You are my Great Grandparents," says Stephen as if this has just come to him.

"Many times over great, you would say son, I assume you were named for me," says the spirit of Stephen. "I assume you were named for me and from I can see you make me proud."

"Thank you sir, I cannot believe I am standing here talking to my great grandparents or should I say my dead great grandparents," says Stephen as he continues to hold Gothia.

"Yes dead but bound here till today," says Stephen as he holds his Rebecca's hand. "Now we are free for I know Rebecca was the victim and much to my regret I did her wrong."

"No my love, I should have told you but I was afraid. Afraid for you and our son, but Stephen I am not free," says Rebecca with a sigh.

"What do you mean? James Smith is gone and we can travel on to our son and many other ancestors since long passed."

"My body Stephen, until it is found and put to rest I cannot leave this world," says Rebecca as a tear forms on her pale, ghostly face.

"We will help you grandmother," says Stephen. "Gothia and I will find it and put you to rest beside grandfather."

"Yes of course we will," says Gothia as she moves to put on a robe. Her heart is pounding. She knows James Smith can no longer hurt her for he has been bound to Hell but Stephen's words still ring in her ears and her heart. He said he loves me, thinks Gothia as she ties her robe. But he just did that to save me. But I know I love him, I was meant for him. If reincarnation real he and I are the reincarnation of the spirits in this room.

"Where do we look?" asks the living Stephen as he wonders why Gothia does not move back over to him. I love her, thinks Stephen, I said so, could it be she does not care for me? I thought she felt the connection. She is the one who has been in my dreams for a long time. We are meant to be together and if she does not know this by now I will convince her. I almost lost her tonight and I will not lose her again.

"Unfortunately we must think as James Smith did," says Gothia. "He was evil but cunning and smart. He would hide Rebecca's body where there was no chance of finding it. I have read your journal and it cannot help for when you died it of course died or quit telling your story."

"Do you recall where you were the night you died?" asked the living Stephen as he moves to Gothia's side and puts his arm around her.

"You do not have to protect me now, you do not have to pretend," whispers Gothia.

"If you knew me as I thought you did you would know I do not play pretend, I am not holding you to protect you. I am holding you because I want to, because you are mine just as my grandmother is to my grandfather," whispers Stephen back/

"I believe our grandson is in love, really in love with my great niece," whispers Rebecca to Stephen.

"I believe you are right, but no one could be in love as we are."

"You might be wrong love, for I see you and I in them," answers Rebecca.

As the spirit of Stephen looks closely at their two living ancestors he knows Rebecca is right. For Gothia is the living replica of his Rebecca and their grandson has his looks and his strong will.

"He will win her, as I won you then," says Stephen.

Gothia knows the spirits are talking about them and she feels herself blushing.

"We need to focus our attention on finding your temporary burial spot and then you and Stephen can join your son," says Gothia as she tries to move the attention away from her and the man next to her.

"I knew it years ago but James Smith played with my mind so long that the memories are intertwined," says Rebecca. "Memories that are all bad."

"Memories love, and now they are gone or will be once we pass on to Heaven, for you have suffered too long not to be an angel," says the spirit of Stephen.

"You too my love," whispers Rebecca as she strokes her husband's face.

"Rebecca this will be hard but it is possible that your burial place is where you were violated by James Smith," says the living Stephen.

"Stephen!" exclaims Gothia. "How can you ask her to remember spots like that?"

"Because I have to, for that is where some one like him would bury her, she more than likely decided to fight him and there in that sport where he planned once more to take her did he kill her," says Stephen as he watches his great grandmother.

"Hush Gothia for he is right, I must recall each place, each time. For the last time I did fight him for my sake and more importantly for my marriage and my family."

"How many times, why did you not tell me, begins the spirit of Stephen but a look from his grandson and Gothia still his voice and questions. "I am sorry, he whispers, "I know you were just protecting our son and me."

"Yes I was but then I thought no more, I will fight him and if I kill him no great loss but he was stronger," says Rebecca.

"Where were you think grandmother, think," says Stephen.

"We were oh where were we," says Rebecca as she pulls at a lock of hair. A habit when she was nervous or upset.

"It will come to you grandmother, maybe if we walk the house with you," says Stephen.

"I want to pray first," says Gothia, "James Smith may be gone but his evil lingers on not only in garage apartment but in this house now."

"A blessing yes a blessing is what we need," agrees Rebecca.

As Gothia begins her prayer a sense of peace envelops the whole room and as they move from room to room the peace expands to cover the whole house.

When the group gets to the garage apartment Rebecca's spirit seems to waiver. As they reach the stairs, she stops.

"Rebecca we must go on, I know this is hard but we must<" says Gothia.

"I know but this room once a retreat for me and my paintings is now a memory of abuse and the degradation he put me through.

"We will bless the room and we will find your body and then once laid to rest with my body we both can move on," says the spirit of Stephen as he takes his wife's arm.

As they move around the garage apartment Gothia continues her prayers. The air seems heavier in this area then the house so Gothia knows this was where most of the abuse took place. Away from the house and rescue.

As they move over to the window seat Gothia notices some thing for the first time.

The wall behind the window box seemed to be loose and the wood was a lighter shade.

"Look here," says Gothia as she points to the wall.

"I see it, it has been changed. Did you ever change it grandfather?"

"No, this room was to be Rebecca's studio. I visited it at first then as things changed between more and more less>"

"I am sorry Stephen," whispers Rebecca.

"No more sorry's love. It is over. We must see what is behind that wall.

"The wall, the window seat. Oh yes I remember," says Rebecca. "James Smith once again wanted me, I was painting and had just put my supplies away in this box. I had painted a picture of him, I made it look as evil as I could and when he saw it he was enraged. I told him I was showing it to Stephen and I was confessing all. He begins to scream and then chant/ I knew then his evil was more than just human, he was a monster, a slave to the devil. He hit me across the face. I pushed him back."

At this point Rebecca stops. The look on her husbands face is one of rage and hurt.

"Stephen remember it is over, we will be free to be together and Gothia and our grandson can become one and love as we did."

"Rebecca!" exclaims Gothia. "This is not about him or me. It is about you and his grandfather."

"She is right Gothia, it is about us. You know it is. I have been dreaming of you long before I met you. Some one in my dreams that seemed so real and if was as if she and I had met before in another life. It was as if we were being drawn together for a reason. The reason our family from the past and the family we will make together in the future," says Stephen as he pulls Gothia to him.

"Stephen," begins Gothia but Stephen stops her by placing his hand over her mouth.

"Later, now we tear a wall apart," says Stephen.

The spirits of Rebecca and Stephen watch as the two young people pull the window seat from the wall. As they pull the boards loose from the wall they see nothing but the outside wall..

"It is empty oh Stephen now what?" asks Rebecca as she leans against her husband.

"No, I know you are here, I just know it," cries Gothia as she looks around. "Wait, maybe it is not the wall maybe it is the window seat."

As they lift the lid of the window seat and pull out all the art paper and supplies they can see that a new bottom had been placed in the box.

As they pull up the false bottom the sight they find horrifies them and yet exhilarates them.

A skeleton lies in the bottom of the box. A scrap of material lie under it and around its neck is a locket.

"It is you, I mean your body," says the spirit of Stephen. "That is the locket I gave you when our son was born."

"Yes now we can bury me beside you and move on."

"I am sorry grandmother it is not that easy. We will need to contact the police and they will need to do an autopsy and then we can have the ceremony and release you," says Stephen.

"How long will this take, I have waited so long." says Rebecca.

"Not long but what will we tell the police. I think they may have a little problem with the truth. Oh my dead grandparents came to us and the evil spirit that was once my grandfather's best friend was the murder. I am not sure that will go over so well," says Stephen.

"That is true but let me think," says Gothia.

"Gothia is a writer she will think of some thing," says Rebecca.

As the trio watch Gothia they can see an idea come to her as she begins to smile.

"I have it, as the new owner of this place I decided to remodel this whole room and when we tore out the window seat it felt heavier than it should have so we inspected it and this is what we found. Stephen you will have to let them know you are the ancestor of the first owners. That way you can get the body released quickly."

"I told you she would think of some thing, oh it will be soon and we will see our son," says Rebecca as she twirls around.

"Now I must call the police, so it might be wise I get dressed and you two go away for awhile," says Gothia. Deep inside she feels happiness not only for her spirit family but for herself and the man who was meant to be with her for ever.

"They will not be able to see us unless they believe in ghosts but we will leave but we will leave together as I will never again be far from my Rebecca," says the original Stephen as he takes his wife's hand and they fade away.

"Gothia we have a long night ahead of us, it will not be easy but I am here and I want you to know I am not going any where," says Stephen as he pulls Gothia to him.

"Are you sure, I mean I do not need protection. James Smith is gone and the house will be cleansed and our or your family can move on to be with their son."

"Gothia I told you I am not going anywhere," and with that Stephen takes Gothia in his arms and kisses her. The kiss is long and hard and very intense.

Gothia feels her whole body shake and she finds herself grasping Stephen's hair and pulling him close to her. The feel of his body is an intense joy and the longer they kiss the more she can feel just how aroused he is.

"Stephen the police," whispers Gothia as Stephen stops for a second.

"I know, god I know but soon nothing will stop me from making love to you," says Stephen as he kisses Gothia once more, the kiss more tender this time but just as enjoyable.

CHAPTER XIV

As Gothia and Stephen watch the police cars and coroners van leave they lean against each other. It had been an all night experience and the first rays of sunlight were filling the sky.

The police were understanding and kind. They took statement from both Gothia and Stephen and had Stephen sign as family once he proved he was family.

The coroner found a crack in the skull of the body indicating blunt force trauma.

The body would be released with in a few days. What the police found interesting was the journal found with the body and the picture of James Smith curled in the bodies' hands.

"Well Gothia soon Rebecca will be laid to rest and she and my grandfather can move on."

"Yes is it not wonderful," says Gothia as she tries not to yawn.

"Oh my love you are exhausted I think I need to get you to bed."

"Stephen!"

"Do not worry Gothia I mean sleep, well this time anyway," says Stephen as he lifts Gothia in his arms and carries her into the house.

Inside the house the spirits of Rebecca and Stephen appear.

" is over and soon we will be released and you two can get on with your lives," says Stephen.

"I will miss you both but am very happy for you," says Gothia as she tries to get Stephen to put her down. Her punch only makes him hold onto her tighter.

"We will miss you but years and years from now we will meet again," says Rebecca.

"Grandson, you will make an honest woman of her before you make love to her right?" asks Stephen

"Stephen!" says Gothia and Rebecca at the same time.

"Yes sir I am as soon as can she will become one of us, she is emotionally but she will be legally. That is if she will have me," says Stephen.

"You are asking me to marry you?"

"Yes Gothia or shall I say Rebecca?"

"I think I like the name Rebecca Edwards."

"Good," says Stephen as he kisses Gothia who will now be his Rebecca long and hard.

EPILOGUE

As Rebecca once Gothia lays the roses on Stephen and Rebecca's grave she sighs.

"What is wrong love?"

"Nothing Stephen I miss them but am happy for them for here they lay with their son," says Rebecca/Gothia as she glances at the grave of Stephen and Rebecca's son. He lived to be over eighty years old and turned out to be as good a man as his father from what she and Stephen read.

"I do to but I know they are smiling at us from heaven."

"Yes they are and for that I am happy"

"Tomorrow is our wedding and tomorrow night I will keep my promise," says Stephen as he pulls Rebecca/Gothia to him.

"Your promise?"

"The promise I made to my grandfather to make you an honest woman then make love to you. It has been hard to wait, but wait I did."

"I found it hard to," whispers Rebecca/ Gothia.

"Oh you rascal," says Stephen as he kisses his future wife.

"Gothia is gone except for her books now I want to be Rebecca Edwards forever."

"Forever it will be," says Stephen as he walks his future bride to his car.

www.ingramcontent.com/pod-product-compliance
Lightning Source LLC
Chambersburg PA
CBHW070808120626
46557CB00002B/760